There are consequences to dreaming, a payment that is always required through the actions and in-actions of the consciousness that wanders through the impossibilities of an illusion, with these impossibilities of a reality authentic as the illusion itself and yet feign as the imagination that diss-illuminates the incomprehensibility of a reality, fractured by an ambitious wonder and or eagerness to explore the unimaginable possibilities of indubitable boundaries.

Therefore...

There is always a line left behind by the unconscious consciousness of a dream, a simple dash of a stroke stretching from within the inconsequentiality of a wonder to the amenability of reality, a temptation of hope and desire, demanding a crossing from one end to the other as an offering of contentment, a satisfaction that comes bathed only in the cheerlessness of a woe.

...

Battles are seductive, war evokes our fascination with spectacle, and there is no greater stage or more dramatic players than on a battlefield.

We are drawn to battles by the lust of the eye, thrilled by a blast from a brass horn as legionnaires advance in glinting armour, or when a king's wave releases mounted knights in a heavy cavalry charge.

the biggest and most important battles by attrition and mass slaughter, not soldiery heroics or the genius of command.

Attrition is believed to be immoral, yet it is how many wars are won. Aggressors defeated the world remade time and again.

CHAPTER ONE

Helel Ben Sahar had wisdom, wisdom enough to know that a head on

Grand battles are an open theatre with a cast of many tens or hundreds of thousands, open armies dressed in red, white or blue, flags fluttering, fife and drums beating the advance.

The thrill of vicarious violence and spectacle is in our nature, thus the misconception of war.

There is heroism in battle, but there are no geniuses in war, war is too complex for a genius to control. To say otherwise is no more than armchair idolatry divorced from the real explanation of victory and defeat.

Whether or not we agree that some wars were necessary and just we should look straight at the grim reality that victory was most often achieved in collision with the forces of Samael would end horrendously for us.

But how do you win a battle when you are not prepared to fight a war.

At the borders of Machonon and Machon, Helel Ben Sahar sent two emissaries to the dreaded Lord of the fifth heaven, *To offer him terms, to buy our passage.*

But the monsters of Machon tore poor *Yamaldor* and *Sintario* limb from limb, and then on a catapult, they swung back their decapitated bodies over the walls, with a scroll tied to each end of the dismembered reading "*No words, only swords.*"

A mad order those powers are, *dogs of conflict and war*, it is the only language that they understand.

At the *Recrudescence wars* of the recreation, 'Zeus' who was then the lord of the sixth heaven Jupiter, refused to surrender the occupancy of the sixth heaven '*Zebul*' to the Entirety.

He dared the *Incorruptibility* to unseat him.

In truth, his pride was not misplaced, for *Zeus* had the *Titans*, the *Thunderbolt* and the *Olympians* as well, who wouldn't fear the king of *Zebul*.

Displeased by the disregard of the Olympian god, the Entirety commanded *Samael* to annihilate the boastful pagan gods and their peoples, to serve as a lesson to all heathen who would dare to question the will of *Shamayim*.

And as it was commanded, *Samael* obeyed.

He and his legion of powers alone entered beyond the Olympian gates, and as they marched into the city of Zebul, we could see from a distance where we waited, a rush of gods, heroes and monsters, charging down towards the gold and white marbles that held the arch of the primordial gates - *The symbol of the sixth heaven.*

Anticipating a calamity, *Michael* interceded the Entirety *"Allow us aid Samael, else he'd be overrun"*. But no, the Entirety refused, "This battle is to become a statement, a warning to all, and I will not have you nor *Helel* interfere. *Have faith the brethren shall overcome*" The entirety assured us.

And as the Olympians drew closer from the North and the legion of powers from the South cardinal, it was only a matter of time before they would both meet at the centre.

And at last when they did, it was not the fight that the Olympians had expected.

The Titans, Hyperion and *Oceanus*, colossals of the Olympians assault were the first to fall on the battlefield, both of them off a single blow by the *Archangel Samael*. And as they fell so too did the gaze of their chief *Zeus*, following them to the drop of dust and blood.

Yet to recover from the shock of their loss, the powers rampaged on the Olympians, the battle was quick and inglorious, *Zeus* and the high Olympians surrendered to the *Archangel Samael* on the day he earned the title "*wrath of God*". All feared the angel that day.

A fear shared by not only the enemy but by the brethren as well.

But that was a time before the fallen would rise, before the balance of all things would come to be tested.

Back at the borders of Machon the Archangel 'Marchosias' asked the Seraphim, Helel Ben Sahar

"How do we enter Machon and emerge without our numbers heavily depleted, for you know *Helel* better than anyone else the malevolent nature of the angel *Samael*... do we surrender *Lilith*" he continued "and request by her an intercession to the *left hand of God,* our passage?"

Impossible, Helel replied, "that would never work", "Then what will" *Belial* asked, speaking for all of the brethren gathered in the council "*BLOOD*"

Helel answered, "only by blood would our passage be bought, only by blood will *Samael* hear us".

"Shall I now ready the army", *Azazel* spoke, "yes" *Helel* consented, "but not all of them" he cautioned, "let only the (4)fourth, the (5)fifth, the (7)seventh and the (9)ninth orders be prepared"

intuiting what the Seraphim intended, *Azazel* called softly to the dragon, "*Helel*! And he said nothing after. "*It is the only way*," the dragon defended, "and I will be with them still, I will not leave them to the monsters alone"

"And I shall be with you also" Belail offered her aid to the Seraphim, but he refused her hand.

"No, you shall be with *Azazel* and the brethren here at Machon, to carry on if the worst should follow, remember, this rebellion is above you or I, it is for all of us... ready the four orders, so that I may speak to them before the march" Helel instructed.

Shortly after, as Helel had commanded, we were gathered at the borders of Machonon, crossing slightly into the red blooded sands of Machon.

Dominions, virtues, principalities and angels, gathered under the banner of the dragon, as he spoke to us;

Sacrifice is an unkindness, never to be demanded of anyone, no matter their quality...

And yet, I would ask you for such unkindness.

We have come far in this rebellion, by blood and sweat, we have conquered Shamayim, Raquia, Shehaqim, Machonon and now we are here, at the borders of Machon, where the monsters of heaven await us.

I look in your eyes and I see that you are afraid, and I understand why, more than you can possibly imagine.

I understand this crippling fear, because I too am afraid, and there is no shame in the admission of this confiscatory emotion... fear.

There is no shame in lacking courage, there is only opportunity to reclaim the lost bravery that this fear wishes to deny us.

We will enter Machon in our thousands, but we may not emerge as much, for the only way that we may win this battle is by the nothingness of death...

And that is the unkindness that I would beg of you, my brethren, to march with me to a death that is more certain than the setting of the sun.

And to the brethren that would choose not to die today...

Go back, rejoin Azazel on the lines, and choose your own days to die, grudges will not be held, desertion shall be no offence, for I have commanded it so.

But to those who will follow me to this death, I will always honour your memory, even though it is to be with me only for a while, for I am too not guaranteed to see the end of this battle nor the end of this rebellion.

CHAPTER TWO.

At the fifth heaven, *Mars*, *Helel Ben Sahar* was dragged through the blood red sands of the city, by the powers of the *Red cathedral*, as they would have done to any pagan god, as they did to **Halirrhothios**, *Poseidon's* son, after he attempted to by violence seduce *Alcippe*, the daughter of *Samael*, the chief of Machon.

There is a saying amongst many peoples "that no one is, or should be above the law", a saying dis-attributed to the angel *Samael* and his flock of powers, for their chief is the one above the nine, the one who is twelve and the one who is among-st the three... the *Demiurge*.

After *Samael* had murdered *Halirrhothios*, the son of Poseidon, the Entirety gave *Poseidon* permission to have *Samael* tried in *Aeropagus* by the *twelve high Greek gods*, as a offering of goodwill, disassociating the *Incorruptibility* from the transgressions of the Archangel.

However, *Samael* was acquitted by the Olympian gods, not because he was innocent of the charges, but rather for fear of his volatile nature, a cup that the Olympians had once tasted off.

Such was the fear and power that the angel commanded, that not even Zeus in an alliance with his brothers Hades and Poseidon could match the power of the *LEFT HAND OF GOD*.

'Seraphim, the burning ones,

the nobles, the most powerful order of the angelic host following their near proximity to the incorruptibility,

they are regarded as the ones of the six,

a title earned by the six wings that they carry upon their vessel,

representing the six planes of consciousness.

They are the brethren obligated with the chanting of the *Trisagion*, which is "*KADOSH, KADOSH, KADOSH*" a chant of celebration and creation to the incorruptibility.

The seraphim are love, light and fire, they are powerful these seraphim's,

but their power is nothing compared to the might of Samael.

Samael, unlike the brethren may not be likened to any of the order of angels,

He may not even be addressed as such, an angel,

for he has no likenesses to the nine, and so he is regarded as the one above the nine, following his physical dissimilarity to the orders of the brethren.

Glaring eyes cover the angel from his head to his toes, with a height so great that it would take an Archangel 500years to cover the entirety of his distance in his true form.

The seraphim, who are the highest order of the angelic host burn in a fire of the six consciousness on their vessel,

but Samael carries a totality of twelve burning wings,

the only being to own as much in all of the heavens and perhaps beyond, thus his title "*the one of twelve*".

Furthermore, the name Samael is mentioned as one of the three names of Demiurge, who is the creator of the universe, alongside the names *Sacklas* and *Yaldabaoth*.

It was rumoured once in the seven heavens that even before Helel Ben Sahar was created and rebelled that Samael had once before creation, sort to rebel against the incorruptibility when he said;

It is I who am god, and there is non apart from me, when he said this he sinned against the entirety and his speech got up to the incorruptibility, and then there was a voice that came forth from the incorruptibility saying, "You are mistaken Samael" which is the god of the blind... and a great silence followed after the speech.

No one is above the law, no one except Samael,

the only celestial permitted to frolic among-st the *angels of sacred prostitution*, among-st, *Ei Sheth Zenunim*, the princess of evil, *Agrat*

Bat Mahlat, the huntress of the air and *Na Amah,* the long haired woman.

A privilege that not even the Seraphim's would dare to request of the incorruptibility.

We call samael an angel of God, but in truth this title is only ceremonial for in all pure conscience, this entity is no angel at all.

At last, Helel Ben Sahar arrived at the bank of the river *'Salsabil'* where he was to be executed by *Agares,* the garroter of the fifth heaven. *Helel* was forced down to his knees, his arms were bound to pillars of stone, each holding a shackle that tightened the Seraphim to the post and then, after he had be secured to the pillars, *Agares* placed an iron collar on Helel's neck as the powers cheered on.

"Any last words" *Agares* asked the Seraphim,

"yes, but they are only three" Helel told the garrotter,

"three is good" Agares replied,

"the fewer they are the better they fall" he told Helel as he turned his gaze to 'Nilaihah' nodding his head, a signal to quiet the crowd,

and so at once *Nilaihah* rang the bells of the three faces of the *Demiurge*,

quieting the crowd,

and as the square grew silent Helel Ben Sahar had these his final words

"I have Lilith" he spoke softly, "I have Lilith" he again retorted, "and if I die here she dies as well" Helel Ben Sahar concluded.

Heaven, what do you imagine when you hear the sounding of the word.

Do you see a paradise filled with beauty and splendour,

where her citizens are skilled in the striking of harps and masterful in the blowing of trumpets,

Do you imagine a place where the angels sing and dance in the bliss of love and grace?

Truly I wish that this here was such a place in this universe, for I would love to be in such a peace...

for here on our own, with these my brethren, such a thing only comes with the wishfulness of a dream.

CHAPTER THREE.

At the mercy of the venom, Samael, Helel could do nothing more but surrender the dream,

the rebellion was over,

the promise was in chains,

the hope that had once rallied us against the entirely, left as quickly as it had possessed us.

And as the powers dragged Helel Ben Sahar to the river Salsabil, shame overwhelmed the princely seraphim, as he could not bear to look upon us the fallen,

he could not bear the fate that would follow, to us who had sworn our immortality to him,

all to perish on the account of his ambition.

But before our defeat at Machon, the fifth heaven, Helel Ben Sahar was invincible.

I remember the battle at the first heaven Shamayim, which aligns with the archangel *Gabriel*.

Helel had asked us to wait at the crystal gates of the first heaven, he said that we needed to place our trust in him,

he told us that he would not ask us to sacrifice our immortality,

if he too wasn't willing to sacrifice his own...

and so at the crystal gates of Shamayim, Helel choose to battle the legions of the first heaven without the fallen,

but only with a handful of his most trusted brethren, *Azazel, Leviathan, Belzeebub, Marchosias and Belial,*

it was madness, it was insane, it was Helel Ben Sahar,

spontaneity was his nature, the distinctiveness that drew us to follow him to the battle of the fallen...

and so we waited at the crystal gates as Helel had instructed, confident and anxious too,

for even with by the powers of a god, a legion of Shamayim worst would not so easily be conquered by less than a handful of soldiers, yet alone two thousand of their best.

Shortly, Helel and his company entered beyond the crystal gates of Shamayim, and as they entered, a cold silence travelled through with the wind, a stillness that held every fallen to a wonder.

And then from the cold and still lingering silence, a deafening roar, shattering the silence, as fire scorched the skies and rains of smoke and ashes poured down upon us.

Among-st the fallen there was an eagerness to go beyond the gates, but none of the fallen disobeyed the Seraphim's command, as none who were instructed to wait by the crystal gates went beyond it.

Obedience is the curse of the divine, it was how we were created, to obey.

At the rallying of the fallen,

before the war,

at a time when the rebellion was only still just an idea,

'*Adramelech*' the first of the principalities to denounce the entirety spoke to us at the twin heavens of Raquia and Shehaqim, by the tower of the conjecture;

"Dare to be free, dare to become your own masters, follow us and be bound to follow no longer the path of any master.

We would erase the hierarchical unkindness that divides the brethren, by the Seraphim Helel Ben Sahar, all shall be one under the banner of the rebellion and no one brethren shall be above the other,

titles shall be earned by labour and not by the favour of how you were made.

Already I have said so much, but the much spoken is far from the promise that the fallen oaths… freedom,

freedom to be who you choose to be and not what you were made to become,

freedom to explore and err and not fear the unfairness of judgement,

freedom to worship as you please and be not condemned to an eternity of damnation.

Freedom to be free.

This is the promise of Helel Ben Sahar as he has sworn it by the light of incorruptibility.

But until that time, when you are free to do as you please,

*now we ask only for the choice of one,
by the duality of another,*

follow us… or not, we will come,

*the fallen shall rise, and Shamayim
will perish.*

"Dare to be free" the simplest of words, with a consequence, far more complicated than our imagination could construct, and yet it was by those words "*dare to be free*" that I chose to rise by the fallen.

At Shamayim, there was a loud roar beyond the crystal gates,

fire in the skies and rain of ashes and soot all about,

but there was no sign of Helel Ben Sahar or of his company.

Despite our admiration and confidence in the quality of the Seraphim,

an unsettledness began to grow within the fallen.

Before the war, many of us had never been in a conflict,

We were not all gallant soldiers like the seraphim prince's, or strong like the archangels, most of the fallen were just basic angels, the lowest of the nine, thus the unsettledness.

There are nine orders of the angelic hosts, we are not all the same.

First there are the Seraphims, the order to which Helel Ben Sahar belongs,

then there are the cherubim,
magnificent beasts of great and mighty
power,

then follows the thrones,

and after them the Dominions,

the virtues,

the powers,

principalities,

the archangels,

and then lastly, the angels,

the lowest of the nine.

*At the gathering of the fallen, to every
order there was a fallen accounted,*

*except the order of the powers, to
which no fallen was accounted,*

As the anxiety grew stronger among-st
the fallen, in the skies, something else
was growing.

A fire covered the Blue and White of
the heavens and then slowly, steadily it
began to twist and turn against the
rotation of the wind, until it became a
vortex of wind, water, and fire.

Soon it drew from its peak to the base of Shamayim, and when it touched on the earth of the first heaven, we heard the screams of thousands, agony and despair.

The fires in the skies soon multiplied, until there were over a hundred spinning flames in the sky.

Such was the power of the inferno, that at the crystal gates we could no longer hear the cries of anguish and pain, but only the whirls of winds and fires.

And although the cries were loud and the fires bright, we still could not see the seraphim,

only hear the frightening growls of a ferocious beast.

Then, after many hours had passed, *Leviathan* came forth, through the burning gates, and as he reunited with the fallen, he proclaimed to us;

"Behold Shamayim is ours, behold the dragon",

and as he spoke to us, we could hear the beatings of a wing greater than the power of one hundred hurricanes,

more tempestuous than the anarchy of the sea,

through smoke, smog and fire, the dragon rose above the chaos,

Helel ben sahar in his full glory, the first time that he had become the dragon, the first time that we beheld him, the transfiguration.

Adramelech at the twin heavens of Raquia and Shehaqim, had told us; *"Follow us or not, the fallen will come and Shamayim will perish"*.

CHAPTER FOUR.

The brethren celebrated the victory at Shamayim,

but Helel ben Sahar retired to Himmelbjerget, the mountain of heaven, to reflect on the wisdom that the archangel Gabriel had left upon him.

As fires rained down from the skies and as the citizens of Shamayim perished, Helel ben Sahar came down, crashing through the lunar cathedral, displacing its cover of timber, plaster and metal too, like an avalanche of fire, pouring like the storms of the oceans.

As the dust and smoke settled,

Helel could clearly see the archangel Gabriel, seated on the *Cathedra, the throne of the first heaven.*

"Hello Gabriel, it has been so long, shall I bow down to the lord of the first heaven?" "No Helel" Gabriel refused,

"but shall I bow down to you, oh ye master of the fallen?" He replied,

"huh" Helel scoffed, "I wasn't expecting to find you here, for I thought for certain that you would have been long gone by now",

"and why would you think that?" Gabriel questioned Helel,

"I think it because I know you well brother, you would rather have words than sharpen the metal of the sword,

and that is why he favours you to run his errands and us other things."

"You're right" Gabriel acknowledged,

"you do know me well, as I too do know you brother, maybe even better than you know yourself",

"is that right" Helel teased the archangel,", "you know it is" Gabriel answered,

"why else have you come to seek me,

if it not be that I alone know you best",

"well it could be because I have started a rebellion against the entirety and also maybe because I just obliterated your heaven,

therefore our meeting was inevitable,

to discuss the terms of your surrender of course."

"Terms?" Gabriel questioned Helel,

"What terms? Our Defences are scattered all over Shamayim,

the city burns as we speak,

the wounded flee to Raquia and the dead carries on,

we have nothing to surrender Helel, nothing to bargain with".

"I wouldn't say that just yet Gabriel" Helel replied,

"the lord of the first heaven is still here, and alive, if I may add,

and I believe that he is a pretty mighty bargaining chip",

"you would hold my life as ransom brother?" Gabriel questioned Helel, "no" Helel replied, "not your life, I threaten something far worse than dying,

but I pray that we do not cross those lines, for I fear that your vessel may not endure the readjustment that would follow".

"What do you want?" Gabriel bluntly asked Helel,

"information" Helel answered, "tell me what I need to know and I would let you run to Raquia, to *Raphael and Anael*".

"What is it, what is this information that you require?"

"I need to know about the entirety, his dwelling place",

"but you know this already Helel, the entirety is always at Zion", Gabriel replied,

"no brother" Helel disapproved,

"the incorruptibility is always at Zion, the entirety only comes to Zion when the incorruptibility wants him there,

I need to know his dwelling place" Helel repeated,

"but why Helel, what brings this sudden obsession with the place of the entirety"

"that is not your concern",

"Do you intend to kill him?" The archangel asked the seraphim,

"can I?" Helel replied,

"you know you can't Helel, but you know that already,

so what do you really want Helel Ben Sahar, what are you running from" Gabriel questioned the dragon,

"who told you that I am running", "I know you well Helel" Gabriel replied,

"and I have seen you run before, as I see you running now, tell me why?"

The archangel urged the seraphim,

and so by the communion of their past and the sway of Gabriel's persistence,

Helel Ben Sahar confessed thus to the lord of Shamayim;

"Before I rebelled, before the ponder of my thoughts had yet become actions,

the entirety requested that I appear at Zion, I was a dutiful servant and so I hurried to him, but when I arrived at Zion, there was a strangeness in the place, the cherubim were absent from their station and no seraphim covered the throne, it was just the entirety and I, and so as he sounded my name, "Helel Ben Sahar", I fell down to my face as we always do before the altar of the Cathedra as he spoke to me;

"Helel, I have seen in your heart an evil, a pride that grows by the wisdom of your knowledge,

a cataclysm to the balance within you.

I wish now to banish you from this place to another of pain and torment, but the incorruptibility thinks not,

*he wishes to let you be, to allow the
potter to finish the clay".*

*With my head bowed down still at the
altar, I requested of the entirety that I
speak;*

*"I feel no evil in my heart or pride in
my wisdom,*

*but if you have seen a corruption
within me that I have been blinded to,*

*I beg thee entirety, intercede the
incorruptibility to remove this evil that
you have seen".*

*"It can not be done" the entirety
refused, "my hands are tied" he told
me,*

"for it is only you seraphim who must remove this destiny yourself".

"And how must I remove this destiny" Helel begged the entirety,

"you can not remove it" the entirety replied,

"For it is only by fulfilling destiny that we are able to be free from it" the entirety concluded.

Helel, Gabriel called softly to get seraphim, "what is this destiny that you must fulfil" he asked,

"you can not understand it brother, even if I try my hardest to explain it to you,

I only require that you tell me where I may find the entirety".

"He is at the space in between spaces",

"that is not a place" Helel refused,

"it is nowhere"

"exactly" Gabriel replied,

"it is nowhere that you have ever been,
but it does exist",

"then tell me how I me how I must get
there" Helel demanded,

"I can't" Gabriel answered,

"all that I can offer you is this;

get to Zion and perhaps the entirety
will come to you"

"that wasn't helpful Gabriel",

"you asked for information and I have offered you the much that I can" Gabriel replied,

"you are the wisest of the Seraphim's, Helel, yet, you have chosen to believe that destiny can be evaded, by running away, it baffles me,

all the death that would follow, all the pain that will come and yet in the end, destiny is always fulfilled,

in your disobedience, you will fall to obedience".

Here take this" Gabriel offered Helel a gift, "what is this?" Helel asked,

"it's a time key" Gabriel replied,

"to a time when there was a man who was just like you, who thought that he could run from his destiny",

"there are no men like me" Helel replied, "yes, there are none like you Helel" Gabriel acknowledged,

"but, go to this time and learn the story of *Oedipus the king of Thebes*, and know what I say is true".

"Oh seraphim, if you would permit it, I wish to be gone now from this place, for the stench of death phases my emotions",

Gabriel requested,

"then go" Helel permitted the archangel,

"but do not go to Raquia or Shehaqim,

for soon they both too shall fall"

"then I shall tell Raphael and Anael to tighten their cities defences as I would now continue to Machonon,

farewell brother" Gabriel concluded, as he spread wide his wings and hurried for Machonon, the sun,

heaven of the archangel Michael.

CHAPTER FIVE.

In the beginning, after Adam, before eve, there was Lilith, Adam's first wife.

"Hurry!" Belial yelled,

"Take me to where you bound the angel with the amulet" and as I led, she followed, until we arrived at the place of the olives, by the walls of the city.

"I don't believe it" Belial expressed shock, upon seeing the angel that I had led her",

"it's been a while Belial" the bounded angel spoke,

"Sansenoi" Belial responded, "yes, indeed, it has been so long",

"you there", Belial then called to me, "go and fetch this one some water", and as she commanded, I obeyed,

but as I left to do as the archangel had instructed, she called back to me once more,

"hey virtue" she called, "do not come back in a hurry",

"Nithael" I responded. "And what is that" Belial asked, "that is my name"

I responded to the archangel, "Nithael, not hey, not virtue,

but Nithael" I told the angel,

"I don't care" she disregarded me, " now go and do as I have instructed" BELIAL yelled.

"You should be nicer to your brethren Belial" Sansenoi advised the archangel, "oh Sansenoi, if I were you, I'd worry more about my own wellbeing"

"Is that so?" Sansenoi replied, "yes it is, but if you cooperate with me, then maybe your wellbeing may be well enough to get you out of this place in one piece",

"ha ha ha", Sansenoi laughed, "your threats never get old Belial",

"I'm glad that you find this hilarious, most people would have soiled themselves already at the sight of me, but not you Sansenoi, I admire your bravery" Belial told the bounded angel,

"shall I begin?" She then inquired of the angel,

"I have nothing to offer you Belial"
"maybe you do or maybe you don't,

I'll leave that for the broken bones to
decide regardless" Belail told
Sansenoi, as she pulled out the amulet
with the inscription upon it, and as
Sansenoi saw the amulet, his eyes
widened, as his gaze fell to his wrist,
and it was at that moment, that he
realised that the amulet had been
pulled off of him.

"So what is it going to be Sansen, are
you going to tell me where the woman
is locked away? Or am I going to have
to break the information I need out of
you?" Belial warned,

"Oh my dear Belial, I have suffered
greater pains than the fracture of

broken bones, break away" Sansenoi
dared the archangel, "break away", he
repeated.

*'Lilith' the woman, had long hair that
hung loose, and it waved like the
serpentine sea, and as she laid in love
with Adam, it smelled to him of
cinnamon, and to Lilith, the hollow
under Adam's arms smelt like apples,
warming in the sun.*

*They were as close as any two could
be, then one day the man Adam said to
Lilith, "get below me",*

*the woman smiled, for she thought that
he was jesting,*

but he said again, "get below me" and the woman did not smile so much again,

and she said, "we were made equally you and I, together,

of the same dust, from all the four corners of the earth"

but Adam said again, "lay below me"

and lilith replied saying, "we were one body and one being, for we were made, he and she together in the incorruptibility's image and we cried equally to the incorruptibility out of our loneliness, and that was why he made us two" but the man Adam said, "only below me", maddened by Adam, Lilith the woman now spoke louder and faster than she did before, as she replied to the man, "together we named every animal that prowls, every fish that cleaves the waters, and every bird that wings the sky, and yet you say to me; get below me?" And so in anger Lilith the woman cried out the ineffable name of the incorruptibility, and the power of the name was so great That it lifted the woman up in the air and she hovered above Adam for a while, and then she was gone, and he saw her no more. Bereft, Adam cried to the incorruptibility, "the woman that you gave me has deserted me".

As I returned with the water which the archangel Belial had requested, the angel Sansenoi that I bound to the olive was unrecognisable,

as Belial had stricken him with the shield of the sword, the branches of the olives, and the fists of her hands, such that only blood could be seen dripping off the face of the angel.

"Water" I spoke softly, announcing my return,

"oh great, just in time" Belial responded, as she hurried for the flask of water and exhausted all of its content on herself, offering non to Sansenoi,

"Go get some more" she again commanded, and as I left, she called back to me again as before, but this time by the sounding of my name, rather than the placement of rank, "Nithael, do not come back in a hurry".

"Adam!" The incorruptibility called to the man, "what troubles you?", "the woman that you gave me has deserted me" Adam answered. On hearing this, the incorruptibility searched the garden for the woman, hoping to find her or that which may have displeased the woman Lilith, and there in the garden, the incorruptibility came upon a vine that he did not plant, that he never did make, and so he asked Adam, "where does this vine come from" and Adam answered, "it was the angel Samael who planted the vine, and there

he and her would be until I have need for the woman, then would she come back to me". And so the incorruptibility looked upon the vine which the angel had planted, and there at the bottom of the tree, he found the seeds of Samael upon the fruits of the vine, whereat the incorruptibility was angry, he cursed Samael and his plant and the woman too, for upon Samael's intrusion in the garden, the woman never belonged to Adam again.

Upset by the meddling of the angel in the garden and the turning of the woman too, the incorruptibility ordered three angels, Senoi, Sansenoi and Sammangelof, to find the woman, the one with the long loose hair that waved like the serpentine sea. And so after many days of searching, the angels found the woman, rocking on the mighty waves of the red sea that already murmured unceasingly of the ghosts of the Egyptians yet to come... They tried to grab her, but over and over again she slipped mockingly through their fingers and her long hair spread through the water like seaweed. But at last one caught her by her sun gold arm and another by her rosy heel and the third by her glistening rippling hair and they held her under the waves until she cried, "let me go" but they did not let her be, as Sammangelof commanded the sea to build them a prison, one strong enough to hold the wind, and the sea obeyed as she built a prison for the angels in the deep, where Lilith the woman with the long black hair was cast away. And so that the place would never be lost to the angels, the ocean asked for the names of the three angels; "so that I shall remember you whenever that you return for your woman" the sea spoke, "Senoi, Sansenoi and Sammangelof" the angels replied and the sea from salt and water and sand, made for each of the angels an amulet with three names written upon them, "whoever returns with this key, shall I release the woman to and no other" the sea concluded.

Upon hearing what the incorruptibility had commanded, Samael fell into a maddening rage, for he loved the woman 'Lilith' so.

With the success of their assignment, the three angels returned to Shamayim, and all was as it had always been, until they arrived at the fifth heaven Machon, where they were intercepted by the angel Samael, who still suffered from the blinding madness of rage, *"where is she?"* He asked the three, *"only the incorruptibility knows"* Senoi replied, "wrong answer" Samael disapproved as he pulled away Senoi's head from his body, to Sammangelof he then turned, "where is she?" He asked, but Sammangelof would not answer, and so he too was without a head on his body, and then to Sansenoi, Samael said nothing, but only; *"take him to the dungeons"* but before his minions could proceed, the entirety intervened, blasting Samael with a power so great that it ripped between *galaxies made and those yet to form, giving the angel Sansenoi a moment to escape, and all who witnessed this moment believed that the angel had perished, for non has heard nor seen the angel since, until...*

As I returned to Belial for the second time with the flask of water, she instructed that I pour some water on Sansenoi who looked dead upon my re-arrival,

"Is he dead?" I asked,

"no! He isn't,

I could never do that to Sansen, believe it or not, Sansen and I are actually good friends" and as Belial said those words, my eyes widened, as I took a long gaze at Sansenoi's face and then slowly returned my sight back to the angel Belial,

"This angel is your friend?" I asked her,

"fine" she grumbled, "don't believe me, you can ask Sansen when he wakes up,

untie him and leave him some water" Belial further instructed, "did you get what you needed" I asked,

"oh yes I did, come we must go to Helel, to share the good news", but then, before we left the place of the olives, there was the sounding of the trumpets, a call to the assembly, "that can't be good" Belial worried,

"come let us go and see why the assembly has been called",

and so together we headed for the assembly of the lunar cathedral to meet with the seraphim Hele Ben Sahar.

CHAPTER SIX.

Behold Shamayim, behold the dragon.

As the fallen rose, Shamayim fell, and all who had doubted once, doubted no more, as the legions of Shamayim fell before the might of the seraphim, Helel Ben Sahar.

Leviathan, led us through the crystal gates as they mangled by the scorching of the fires,

we entered Shamayim singing praises to the invincibility of the dragon, a tribute to him, for his victory over the first of the heavens,

although a small step, a step in the right direction.

"Gather the wounded, bury the dead" the angel Nelchael instructed, as Helel Ben Sahar had commanded.

Although the dragon did not speak to the fallen after the conquest of Shamayim, instead he retreated to Himmelbjerget, the mountain of heaven, and he remained there, on the hill, staring at the sun, *Machonon*.

As we dug through the bodies of the dead searching for the wounded, I found someone, alive, he had an amulet on his right arm, and on this amulet was written the names of three angels, "*Senoi, Sansenoi and Sammangelof,*" and i knew these names, I remembered their story.

At once I pulled the angel out of the rubble of the dead and dragged him through a mud of blood, to the shade of olives by the walls of the city,

I offered him some water and he accepted the drink;

"What is your name?" I then asked the angel, but he did not reply, he seemed distraught, absent minded and agitated,

but then again who wouldn't be, after witnessing the events in the first heaven.

Quickly I bound his arms to his feet and then anchored him to the branch of an olive, confident that he was secured I hurried to the lunar cathedral where I had seen the archangel Azazel earlier.

As I arrived at the threshold of the palace, I saw Azazel at the gardens of the cathedral, sharpening knives and testing metals, "Azazel" I called to him, as I hastened to where his station,

"what do you want" the archangel spoke bluntly to me, "I found something" I told the angel, "take it to Belial" he replied, "but I think it could be valuable sir", "take it to Belial", the archangel insisted, as he was more interested in his metals than on the value of my find,

"and where could Belial be?" I asked Azazel, "follow the disorder, you'd find her closest to the chaos".

Belial, the archangel of lawlessness, deceptively beautiful in appearance, soft in voice and inexpressibly wicked in everything else.

I was hesitant to find the archangel,

not only because I was afraid to meet with her for the first time,

but also because I was absolutely terrified of her unpredictable nature,

a reputation of wariness that precedes her.

But then by cursed luck, as I turned to the east, over the river of ice and glass, I found her, sitting on a heap of the dead, singing the *"Dies Irae" The day of wrath*;

Dies irae, dies illa, solvent saeculum in favilla, teste david cum sibylla.

Quantis tremor est futurus, quando
iudex est venturus, cuncia stricta
discussurus.

Tuba murum spargens sonum per
sepulcra regionum, coget omnes ante
thronum.

Mors stupebit et natura, cum resurget
creatura, uudicant responsura.

Liber scriptus proferetur, in quo totem
continetor, unde mudud iudicetur.

Iudex ergo cum sedebit, quidquid latet
apparebit, nil inultum remanebit.

Qud sum miserntunc dicturus, quem
patronum rogaturus, cum vix iustus sit
securus.

Rex tremendae maiestatis, qui salvandos gratis salva me, tons pietatis".

As I arrived at the spot where the archangel sang the irea, she ended her singing and stared at me as she said;

"Does my singing offend you?"

"No" I replied, "it is a song befitting of the dead", "then why do you look so displeased", "this is how I always look", I responded, "Ha ha", Belial laughed, "You're not a very good liar my friend", "no I'm not" I confessed, "it's the corpses" I stuttered, "what about them?" Belial asked, shrugging her shoulders as though she was oblivious of the unsettling nature of her posture upon the bodies of the dead, "are you being funny?", I disconcertingly asked, she chuckled softly and replied, "no I'm not trying to be funny, what is wrong with the corpses? ", "You're sitting on them" I told her, "that's what is wrong", "and why is it wrong for me to sit on the dead?" , "it's wrong because they're dead" I answered, "exactly", Belial hollered, "they're dead, and they don't mind if my arse is on their dead faces, heck they may even enjoy my arse grinding on their faces."

"... come closer" Belial then whispered to me,

and as I did, she put a finger to her lip shushing as I drew nearer to her,

"listen", she then said,

"don't tell anyone that I said so she advised,

we wouldn't want to have certain brethren in the rebellion feeling unworthy",

"of course not, I shall tell no one of the secrets you tell me", I whispered back to the angel, "what is it" I asked her,

"You see these brethren, the ones that I'm sitting on?

"Yes I do", I urged her to continue,

"they're *Grigori*, you know *the watchers*, the daughters of men watchers",

she wiggled her brows, as mine furrowed, "what about them?" I asked her, "well everyone knows already", she replied, "but still don't tell anyone, I'm sitting on them, to honour their dying wish",

"are you serious", I accused the angel,

"so these angels asked you to sit on them before they died",

and as she had done earlier, she put a finger to her lip shushing, "not so loud", she cautioned, "but yes, that's the truth,

some parts of it anyways,

and please do wipe off that horrible judgmental impersonation of god that you have on your face, because it makes me want to stab you in the eye", belial threatened.

"May I please just deliver my message to you and leave",

"why? Are you in a hurry", belial asked, "yes I am in a hurry",

"You're still a bad liar" the archangel laughed, "go ahead", she then permitted, "what do you want",

"Azazel sent me, I found someone",

"and how does that concern me, take them to a cell or put them out of their misery...,

oh", belial paused, "so that's what you need me for,

to help you put them out of their misery, yes? Squeamish virtues, you who are regarded as the embodiment of unyielding spiritual and physical courage,

but you're all just..., well I think you know what you are".

"What are you talking about", I expostulated at the archangel,

"Do you ever stop talking long enough to hear the other person speak?

I don't need you to come kill anyone, thank you very much,

I need you to come with me to see an angel that I found on the field,

that had this on him", I showed belial the amulet with the writings on it, and as she read the names of the three angels inscribed on the amulet her eyes brightened and her voice flaked as she asked,

"where did you find this",

"at the meadows, just before the cathedral", I replied "and the angel you pulled this off",

"He's alive, I safeguarded him to the branch of an olive, by the walls of the city, "an olive branch?" Belial mused,

"take me to him".

CHAPTER SEVEN.

Raquia, the heaven which aligns with the archangel *Raphael* and *Shehaqim* which aligns with *Anael*, were next on the fallen's path to the entirety, and although excitement towered among-st the fallen, Helel Ben Sahar showed no eagerness to engage the twin heavens of Raquia and Shehaqim, as he remained on top of the mountain Himmelbjerget, pondering on a thought.

Azazel was the only angel permitted to go up to the dragon, and after much waiting, as the dragon did not come down, Azazel went up to Helel Ben Sahar on the mountain, and as he arrived at the top of it, he at once questioned the seraphim;

"What is wrong?"

"Gabriel", Helel answered,

"What about Gabriel? " Azazel asked,

"he said to me at the lunar cathedral;

that from our disobedience we shall fall to obedience.

Those his words exactly", helel told Azazel,

"but that is not true",

Azazel replied, "we have broken vows, sacred vows,

that even the entirety dare not ponder,

the incorruptibility is bound to the bond of the brethren and must not yield to any interference or corruption,

hence the title,

"everything that you have just said", Helel replied,

"were the lessons that the entirety was by duty compelled to mould in us as instructed by the incorruptibility, anyone can become corrupted Azazel, every being has a corruption within them,

whether it be called a flaw,

a shortcoming,

or a pride,

it is the definition that we give to these failings that differs from one to the other."

"I have never seen you like this Helel",

"and I have never felt like this either, not even when that fool *Adam* was created", "Ha" Azazel chuckled,

"so what do you intend to do now",

Azazel asked,

"there is a path, but it is Gabriel's path", Helel replied as he pulled out the time key that the archangel Gabriel had gifted him for Azazel to see,

"Is that what I think it is?" Azazel marvelled,

"yes it is", "and where does it lead?"

"Gabriel didn't say, only that to this time, I shall find a story that I need learn",

"And you do not suspect a trap?" Azazel warned,

"no, I don't, but if it were to be a trap, I can handle well my own,

"I know you can", Azazel confirmed.

"But if you leave now, you would not be with us, when we enter the twin heavens of Raquia and Shehaqim", "yes", Helel acknowledged,

"shall I stay behind, until the siege is over?" Helel offered,

"against Raphael and Anael? Please! We would be fine, go to this place and find the answers that you seek, and then when you are whole, come back to us", Azazel told the dragon, and he spoke no more as he left Helel Ben Sahar at Himmelbjerget to prepare the fallen for the march ahead, and as the archangel descended the mountain,

the seraphim Helel Ben Sahar, unshielded the key that the angel Gabriel had given him, and with it he entered the time that the archangel had intended,

the time of *Oedipus Rex*, the king of *Thebes*. And so the dragon became witness to the following events;

A plague has stricken Thebes.

The citizens gather outside the palace of their king Oedipus, asking him to take action.

Oedipus replies that he had already sent his brother-in-law Creon to the oracle at Delpi, to learn how the city must be saved.

Soon Creon returns with a message from the oracle;

"The plague will end, when the murderer of Laius, the former king of Thebes is found and expelled,

for the murderer is within the city."

Oedipus questions Creon about the murder of Laius, who was murdered by thieves on his way to consult an oracle,

Creon narrates the events of the past to Oedipus and concludes the tale by informing Oedipus that only one fellow of Laius's company survived the attack.

Oedipus promises to solve the mystery of Laius's death,

vowing to drive out the murderer,

and so the king of Thebes sent for Tiresias, the blind prophet...

soon the prophet arrives and Oedipus questions him on what the oracle can tell about the former kings murder.

Tiresias responds cryptically to Oedipus, lamenting his ability to see the truth,

when the truth only brings nothing but pain.

At first Tiresias refuses to tell Oedipus what he knows, so the king curses and insults the old man, going so far as to accuse him of the murder of Laius.

These taunts provoke Tiresias into revealing that Oedipus himself is the murderer of the late king Laius.

Naturally Oedipus refuses to believe Tiresias's accusation,

he accuses Creon and Tiresias of conspiring against his life and also he charges Tiresias with insanity,

he asks why the prophet did nothing when Thebes suffered under a plague before.

At that time, a Sphinx held the city captive and refused to leave until someone answered her riddle.

Oedipus brags that only he was able to solve the riddle.

Tiresias defends his calling as a prophet, noting that Oedipus's parents found him worthy.

At the mention of his parents, the king who grew up in the distant city of Corinth, asked how Tiresias knows his parents,

but Tiresias refused to answer, but before he leaves, he puts forth one last riddle;

"the murderer of the late king would turn out to be both father and brother to his own children and the son of his own wife.

Oedipus threatens Creon with death, for conspiring with the prophet Tiresias.

Jocasta, Oedipus's wife, also the widow of the late king arrives at the palace and questions why both men spoke so loudly, Oedipus explains to Jocasta that the prophet has charged him with the murder of Laius,

Jocasta replies that all prophecies are false, as proof she notes that the Delphic oracle once told Laius that he would be murdered by his own son, when in fact his son was cast out of Thebes as an infant and Laius was murdered by a band of Thieves.

Her description of Laius's murder sounds familiar to Oedipus and so he asks further questions.

Jocasta tells him that Laius was killed at a three way crossroad, just before Oedipus arrived at Thebes.

Stunned, Oedipus tells his wife that he fears he is the one that murdered Laius, he tells Jocasta that long ago, when he was still the prince of Corinth, he overheard the mention, at a banquet, that he was not the true son of the king and queen.

He therefore traveled to the oracle at Delpi who refused to answer him, but he did tell him that he would murder his father and sleep with his mother.

Hearing this Oedipus fled his home never to return, it was then, on the journey that would take him to Thebes that Oedipus was confronted and harassed by a group of Travellers who he killed in self defence.

The skirmish occurred at the very crossroad where Laius was killed.

Afraid that the oracle may be correct, Oedipus sends for the man who survived the attack at the crossroad as Creon had informed him earlier of the survival,

the man a shepherd by profession soon arrives and Oedipus in fear hopes that he would not be identified by the man as the murderer of the king.

Meanwhile outside the palace a messenger approaches Jocasta, he tells her that he has come from Corinth, to tell Oedipus that his father Polybus is dead and that Corinth has decided to ask Oedipus to become king and rule in his father's place.

Jocasta rejoices at the news, convinced that Polybus's death from natural causes has disproved the prophecy that Oedipus would kill his father.

At Jocasta summons, Oedipus meets with the messenger from Corinth, he is told of the news of his father's death and he rejoices, he now feels much more inclined to agree with the queen in deeming prophecies worthless and viewing chance as the principle governing the world.

But while Oedipus finds great comfort in the fact that one half of the prophecy has been disproved, he still fears the other half, the half that claims "he would sleep with his mother."

The messenger remarks that Oedipus need not worry because Polybus and his wife Merope are not Oedipus biological parents.

The messenger a shepherd by profession knows first hand that Oedipus came to Corinth as an orphan.

One day he was tending to his sheep when another shepherd approached him carrying a baby, with his ankles pinned together. The messenger took the baby to the royal family of Corinth and they raised him as their own, that baby was Oedipus.

Oedipus asks the messenger who the other shepherd was, and the messenger answers that he was a servant of Laius. Oedipus commands that this shepherd be brought forth to testify, but Jocasta, beginning to suspect the truth, begs her husband not to seek more information and so she runs back into the palace. Shortly after the shepherd from Thebes arrives, Oedipus interrogates him, asking him who gave him the baby, the shepherd is reluctant to disclose anything and so Oedipus threatens him with torture and death.

Finally he answers that the child came from the house of Laius.

Questioned further, he answers that the baby in fact was the child of Laius himself and that it was Jocasta who gave him the infant, ordering him to kill it, as it had been prophesied that the child would one day kill his parents, but the shepherd pitied the child and decided that the prophecy could be avoided if the child were to grow up in a foreign city far from his parents. The shepherd therefore passed the boy to another shepherd in Corinth, the messenger from Corinth.

Realising who he is, and who his parents are, Oedipus screams that he sees the truth and he flees back into the palace where he was met by a servant, who describes to him scenes of pain and suffering, Jocasta has hanged herself and Oedipus finding her dead, pulled the pins from her robe and stabbed out his own eyes.

Oedipus then emerged from the palace, bleeding and begging to be banished,

He begs Creon to send him away from Thebes and to look after his daughters, Antigone and Ismene.

Creon covetous of royal power is all too happy to oblige,

Oedipus is exiled and Creon becomes king.

Helel Ben Sahar is touched by the tragedy of Oedipus who tried to escape his destiny but still fell upon it.

Helel wonders; "was this what Gabriel intended to show me",

unsatisfied with the events that he had witnessed, Helel searches for Oedipus, and soon he finds him with Theseus,

He requested for a moment with the blind prince of Corinth, the former king of the Thebes, and verily his request was granted.

"Hello I'm Helel Ben Sahar",

"and I'm Oedipus", the blind prince replied, "how may I help you" Oedipus offered,

"I have heard your story" Helel replied,

"you were helpless against destiny,

in running away from its grip, you ran towards her, you could never had escaped the potter,

so I have come to ask you one question only",

"Go ahead" Oedipus approved.

"As you sit here now, blinded, lost, stripped of all that you were by the unkindness of fate,

if you were to live this life again, would you still fight your destiny, even though you know that all your struggles would end then as it has now, in tragedy?"

"Yes I will fight such a destiny, so that it may never be fulfilled",

Oedipus answered, "but you have fought it once and this is the result",

"no Helel, I did not disagree with my destiny, when I was told of it by the oracle at Delphi, I did not oppose it,

I ran from it, there is a difference in running and fighting"

"Helel", Oedipus then called to the seraphim, "if I am reincarnated to this fate in another life, I will fight such a destiny and longer run from it.

Tell me Helel, are you running or fighting?"

Helel ben Sahar took a deep long breath and answered, "both, I am fighting and running."

"I have been a warrior once" Oedipus revealed,

"and I know that one can not run and fight at the same time,

you have to choose one above the other,

or fate would make that choice for you." "Thank you for your time", Helel appreciated Oedipus's honesty,

"if you request it, I can restore your sight",

"gratitude", Oedipus replied,

"but no", he refused,

"this was how I was intended to live and die,

and i pray not to see again, until I see the four corners of the grave"

and as Oedipus concluded, so too did Helel ben Sahar rise from his seat and return to the time from whence he came.

CHAPTER EIGHT.

The march to the twin heavens, *Raquia and Shehaqim* was long and uneasy,

It took us three days to arrive at the twin cities which align with the archangels *Raphael and Anael* respectively.

The battle of the twin heavens presented the fallen with a complication,

as one heaven could not be taken without drawing resistance fire from the adjacent heaven,

to take Raquia, Shehaqim must be engaged at the same time as well,

vice versa, as both heavens must fall simultaneously.

The task was daunting, for Helel Ben Sahar was not amongst the fallen at the siege of Mercury and Venus,

only Azazel, the archangel in charge.

We set up camp at the valley of the fallen kings,

a place in heaven where the souls of all the lords who have lived and died, good and maybe some evil reside,

a haunted place, filled by the brokenness of dreams never achieved and satisfactions that were never contented,

a haunted place.

Azazel gathered the high celestials to a tent at the valley of the fallen kings, to discuss our strategy,

for the B*attle of the Conjecture.*

"When would Helel return", Leviathan asked,

"he didn't say", Azazel replied,

"and that is the only answer that I will offer to any who would ask of the whereabouts of the dragon,

So please brethren, let us focus on the task before us, and not on the whereabouts of Helel.

Helel has proven himself to the fallen, to all of the brethren,

this is our chance to prove our worthiness to the seraphim,

so let our thoughts be strident on the fall of the conjecture."

"What is our strategy?" Belzeebub asked,

"divide and conquer" Azazel replied,

"we must enter both cities from both cities gates,

if we choose to enter Raquia first and Shehaqim later,

the archers of Shehaqim would rain down fire upon us and we may not endure.

But if we enter Raquia and Shehaqim by the divide, at the same time, both cities would have to mind their own, and if we act swiftly enough, we could be able to put down the twin lords of the twin heavens at the cathedral, Raphael and Anael,

forcing their forces to surrender, thus handing us the opportunity to evacuate the second and third heaven,

paving our way to Machonon.

It is a simple strategy" Azazel told the brethren,

"But it is not," Belial objected. "The twin legions of the Conjecture,

wouldn't just allow our forces to stroll into the twin cathedral,

and if we go in through the cover of the city,

they will still open fire upon us from the walls of the city",

"yes, I have thought about that", Azazel replied,

"Leviathan and I would lead the opening charge through the gates of Raquia and Shehaqim simultaneously and from there push backwards any resistance to the cities conjecture,

where I am certain that reinforcements from both cities' legions would meet us to halt our advance.

At the conjecture, belial would enter Raquia to support our forces and Belzeebub would enter Shehaqim to do the same, Leviathan and I would give you both a slight chance to slither through the lines,

from where you would both make haste for the cathedral to engage Raphael and Anael.

I have no doubt in your quality,

but still I must ask you, can you take Raphael and Anael? "

"I can take them both", belial boasted,

"we can take them", Belzeebub confirmed, "very well then", Azazel spoke,

"Leviathan" he then called, "do you have anything further to add?"

"No, nothing", he replied, "then let us prepare for battle" Azazel concluded.

The battle of the twin heavens was to become our initiation to the war,

as it was our first involvement in the battle of the rebellion, and we were all prepared.

However, before the battle of the twin heavens the fallen had no ranks, only strength in numbers, but Azazel corrected this disadvantage as he structured the fallen into a legion of five thousand strong, with a *primus pilus* assigned to every *cohort* and a *centurion* to every *Centuria* and the centurions to the *legions* and the legions to their *commanders*.

At the valley of the fallen kings, Azazel appeared to speak to the rebellion;

Helel Ben Sahar is not here with us at the moment,

and I am to take command of the fallen until his return.

I have no intention of losing this war at the passing of my first baton,

and so I will not tolerate any form of weakness among-st the brethren.

I am aware that many in our ranks know little or nothing at all of warfare,

but that is not an excuse to ill-perform.

You have chosen to follow the dragon and you have sworn your immortality to him,

so now, there is no going back, there is only success or death, and I wish to keep us all alive.

There are swords to be sharpened and armour to be fitted,

let those who can not fight do other things, and let those who can... prepare. "

Azazel was a first ranking centurion of the first ranking cohorts, "*primus pilus*" in the *recrudescence wars of the recreation,*

He participated in the councils of war with the entirety and hosts of the military tribunes and legion commanders.

The fiercest fighter we had, only bettered by perhaps, Helel Ben Sahar.

As Azazel concluded his address to the fallen, Belzeebub stepped Forward and instructed as follows;

Hear me, these names I mention now, the cohorts that will make the division of the legions, they will pick of those willing to fight and assign to each legion sixty centurions' that would make the six thousand of the legion, and to every legion a commander, until all or none can be assigned any further, and thus the names;

Berith, Lauviah, Marou, Salikotal, Tocalor, Basasael, Forneous, Gressil, Mammon, Murmir, Nelchael, Plenex, Adramelech, Puson, Raum, Sonneillon, Sytri, Verrine...

It took us three days to assign every fallen to a Centuria and every Centuria to a centurion,

and at the end, we were a solid twenty five thousand strong,

five legions mighty.

And to the legions, her commanders; *Azazel, Leviathan, Belzeebub, Marchosias, and Belial,*

our numbers enough to strike fear and doubt in the hearts of any mortal army,

but our war was not against those of flesh and blood, but of the divine,

and to them our numbers were frail and fickle.

I was assigned to Azazel's command, under the supervision of *Basasael,* his command, the first to enter Raquia.

Belial met with me at the armoury, where I had gone to sharpen my sword and be fitted to Armour.

"Look at you all armoured up"

belial teased, "to whom have you been assigned?" She then inquired,

"Basasael" I replied, "and he to Azazel,

"oh dear", Belail wailed,

"good luck virtue" she then concluded,

"what is that supposed to mean" I quickly replied,

"nothing" belial smiled as she responded,

"I'm only wishing you the best",

"well, if that's the truth,

then thank you for your concern" I told the archangel,

"and good luck to you as well",

"oh please" the archangel jeered, "have you seen my command Nithael? " she boasted, "

we don't need luck, I have the best of the angels that can handle the metals of the sword.

Don't die out there virtue" she continued, "for I have gotten used to sensing your presence, little virtue",

unsure how I was to respond to the angels unusual comment,

I simply nodded my head in acknowledgment and walked away to my station.

At the rising of the sun, war.

Leviathan and Azazel marched their legions to the gates of the twin cities,

and so the battle for the second and third heaven began.

The days that we lost organising the ranks, served as an advantage to the opposition, as they reinforced the cities defences, mounting more artillery on the walls and more men at the gates.

At the gates it took Azazel and Leviathan longer than they had anticipated to break-in to the cities, as fire rained down from above and many brethren perished,

but soon we were In and we revealed, *swinging the sword and stabbing wildly, screaming and roaring, goring and bleeding, weeping and killing.*

At the tower of the conjecture, Azazel commanded that the signal for reinforcement to Belial and Belzeebub be sent, and as they both received that command, they made haste to the conjecture,

with belial reinforcing Azazel and Belzeebub joining Leviathan on the right, which was the entrance through Shehaqim.

We fought for hours,

but there were no cracks in the enemy's line as expected.

Belial desperate to get through the bodies of spears and armour, fought her way to the right flank of the conjecture, to Leviathans command,

"There is no way through", she yelled, hoping that Leviathan would hear her, and he did,

"where is Belzeebub? " Leviathan replied,

"what? He's supposed to be with you" belial replied,

"he was, but I haven't seen him since after the reinforcements",

"maybe he got through", the archangel belial suggested,

"Impossible" Leviathan disagreed,

"Have you seen this line? Nobody is getting through, not this way at least",

"what do I tell Azazel", "we hold" Leviathan answered, "until it is over to whatever end."

"Find another way, we would hold the line" ,

"I don't know another way" belial replied, "then find someone who does and hurry, we're running out of men."

"Fuck!" Belial cussed, "how do I cross these damned lines" she thought, as a voice from the chaos shouted her name,

"belial!, but the archangel did not notice the yell,

belial! Again the voice screamed, this time louder than before, and as the archangel heard the sounding of her name she turned around slightly to know who it was that calls her,

and as she turned it was I, Nithael,

Azazel had sent me from the left flank to find belial and order her back to the left flank to help hold the lines,

"you" belial yelled, "You're not dead" she told,

"no I'm not, we need help on the left, my unit is breaking, we would not hold for long"

I told the angel, " report it to Basasael",

" he's dead",

"well that's no surprise, he's a terrible with the sword",

"what?" Nithael blared, "you should have told me before the march",

"but I did, remember when I wished you good luck, that was my own way of saying that you may not survive",

"how does that even make sense" Nithael angrily retorted,

"you may express your disgruntled emotions later,

because now I need to find someone who knows another way into the twin cathedral",

"I do" I told the angel,

"really? Where is he?"

Belial excitedly replied,

"it's me" Nithael answered,

" I know the way into the cathedral,

"you fantastic little virtue" belial rejoiced, " take me there now",

" But what about my unit and Azazel's command?"

"That's Azazel's problem, let's go she urged me",

"Okay follow me" I told the archangel as I led her to the cathedral.

Before I rebelled against the entirety, Raquia was my home,

I served under the archangel Gressil as an assistant to the cathedral's librarian,

and so naturally I knew ways in and
out of the cathedral like the back of my
hand.

I led belial through *the forgotten paths
of the narrow brightness*,

a pathway built by the pagan god
Osiris, who was once the master of
Raquia and Shehaqim,

before the recrudescence wars,

before we claimed the third heaven
from the Egyptian god.

He built the channel to smuggle souls
that the favoured,

those deemed unworthy of the afterlife,
without the notice of *Anubis*, into
Shamayim.

Few angels know this path,

even I too only came across it by accident,

soon Belial and I were through,

The path led us to the cathedral court, which was faintly guarded, as many of the heavens forces were deployed to defend the conjecture.

"What's the plan" ,

I asked Belial,

"Belzeebub and I were supposed to take each of the lords of the twin heavens and persuade them to surrender",

" but Belzeebub isn't here" I told belial,

"no, he's not,

but you are",

"NO! I do not possess the quality to engage an archangel ",

I told belial,

"just hear me out" she pleaded,

"I'll take Raphael and, or Anael,

I'll take whoever is at the cathedral,

all that I need from you Nithael is to defend my back against any surprise reinforcements,

Can I trust you to do that?"

"But Raphael and Anael are archangels" I replied,

"I'm just a virtue, this could end very badly for me, for us, "it won't" belial assured me,

"can you trust me?"

She asked me softly,

and so I pondered for a moment by a deep long breathe and then "yes" I replied to the archangel, "I can"

"thank you" she replied,

"And can I trust you as you say that you trust me, to watch my back?" Belial continued,

and to that inquiry, I had not the answer, for I did not even trust my quality wholly to defend myself absolutely on the battlefield, talk more of an archangel,

" Nithael! Can I trust you?" Belial resounded,

"yes you can"

"good, I never doubted you, stay on my heel she instructed,

as we headed for the threshold of the cathedra.

On our way to the cathedra, we encountered few obstacles,

nothing the archangel couldn't handle,

and so shortly we arrived at the throne room of the cathedral, "*the cathedra of the conjecture*",

"remember our deal, watch my back and I'll do the rest"

belial spoke and I nodded to her in acknowledgment to her words, as she made for the cathedra doors,

and I remained behind, the guard of the guard.

And as she pulled open the cathedra doors, Raphael, Anael and Belzeebub were in the room.

"Why does Helel Ben Sahar, continue to insult us with such unworthiness"

Anael spoke, "shall he not come to us himself?

Why suffer us with the unworthy. "

"What happened to Belzeebub" belial asked,

"his quality was lacking" Raphael answered, "is he dead?" Belial further inquired,

"very much so" Anael told,

" hmm- the archangel belial worried,

"would you like to surrender sister"

Anael asked belial, the archangel of lawlessness,

"you both forget who it is that I am" belial threatened, as she charged onward towards the lords of the twin heavens, unyielding her sword as she drew closer,

and so the battle of the three archangels began at the twin cathedral.

Back at the conjecture, the legions of the rebellion were stretched thin by the forces of Raquia and Shehaqim,

so thin that the lines barely held.

Leviathan was drunken by the glory of battle and so he did not notice that the flanks were about to crumble.

"Call for reinforcements" Azazel commanded,

"order Marchosias to come with a quarter of his command and reinforce the centre,

for if the centre breaks, the army would be divided and we would all be dead.

Where is Leviathan? "Azazel then asked, "he has gone mad" Barbados answered, "he advances without the line, he doesn't listen"

"Leave him to me" Azazel replied, as he hurried to Leviathans command.

Shortly, Azazel found Leviathan further ahead on the battlefield, than the men that he commanded,

"Leviathan! Azazel shouted, but the angel did not answer, Leviathan! Again Azazel called, but still the archangel did not answer,

frustrated, Azazel ascended to where the archangel raged, joining him in battle, stabbing and guarding the archangel,

Leviathan! Azazel then called for the third time, "yes" Leviathan answered, "are belial and Belzeebub through" he asked Azazel,

"I don't know" Azazel replied,

"but they will find a way, I'm sure of it"

Azazel continued,

"but that's not why I'm here,

"Why are you here?" Leviathan asked Azazel,

"you're too far off the line, we need you to compensate the army, I need you to return back to the flank, your men need you, if the lines break we are all dead.

" Leviathan! Azazel called softly,

"I need you to slow down" and for the first time since he lost himself in battle, Leviathan took a moment and looked around the battlefield, realising that he had been carried away,

"Azazel" Leviathan then called,

"we need to go back to the lines, and call for reinforcement"

"I already did brother"

"Okay let's go back" Leviathan conceded to Azazel's reason.

At the cathedra, belial held her own well against the lords of the twin heavens,

but she was yet at a disadvantage,

for they were two and her one.

I thought to go and assist the archangel of lawlessness,

but my courage was lacking,

so I stayed back at the threshold as she had instructed,

observing the struggle of the archangels at a distance safe enough to evade.

As the conflict waged, belial managed to architect an advantage from an usual skill of sword,

cutting Anael deep at his thighs, just above the knee, temporarily immobilising the archangel, causing him great pain,

"it's just you and I now Raphael" belial told the lord of Raquia, "heal me brother" Anael yelled, writhing in pain,

"of course" belial realised,

"how stupid we have been,

no wonder we can not break the conjecture...

Raphael, the archangel of healing" belial called to the archangel, "you have been resuscitating what we cut down, we would never win this battle unless you are put away"

then belial took a moment to steady herself,

and then raised her sword,

pointing the blade at Raphael,
"you overestimate yourself sister"

Raphael responded,

"maybe" belial replied,

"let's find out" she concluded as she charged at Raphael,

striking blow, after blow, after blow,

until the lord of Raquia lost his footing slightly and belial quick as she was, stabbed him deep in the heart,

killing him at the spot.

No! Anael cried as the pain of watching Raphael murdered overwhelmed the discomfort of the cut on his thigh.

Anael struggled to regain his footing and then once on his feet,
he threatened belial with death,

"you will die here whore"

"Do you praise your god with that mouth?" Belial mocked Anael,

as he drew closer to her swinging out of desperation, lacking in skill and discipline, and so belial cut him down again on his other thigh, forcing Anael to his knees,

"do it" Anael urged the archangel,

"end my life"

"no" belial refused, "you don't deserve to become a martyr, you do not deserve the title of lord, nor the rank of an archangel, you are weak as any mortal could be, though I believe strongly, than if a man be brave enough, still he would make you bleed" belial concluded,

as she severed all six wings of the archangel Anael,

stripping him of all the consciousness that makes him a brethren of the order and then she turned to him and spoke in a tone gentle like the tender woollens of a sheep, "run."

Nithael, belial then called to me,

I hurried to her and as arrived at her call, she fell to my arms,

"I have never seen anything like that before"

I confessed to the archangel,

"well, I'm full of surprises" belial struggled to speak, drained from her encounter with the twin lords, "tell me what you need" I urged the archangel,

" lay me down" she answered and I did, "take those" she pointed to Anaels wings, which she had severed, "fly them over the conjecture, and let his legions see them as they fall, for they will surrender at the realisation that their lord has fallen" "and Raphael?" I asked belial,

"His men can no longer heal, they soon shall realise that their lord has fallen as well.

And as Belial had predicted the legions of the twin heavens surrendered to us, when they realised that their lords had fallen. Helel ben Sahar was not with us at the battle of the conjecture, yet it was his name that the fallen proclaimed through the heavens of Mercury and Venus. "Helel Helel, Helel, Helel…"

CHAPTER NINE.

At the borders of Machonon and Machon, after Helel Ben Sahar had rallied us by the speech of sacrifice, he marched into the fifth heaven mars,

and as he led the fallen followed, marching to a certain death.

As we encountered the powers at Machon, before I unshielded my sword,

I found myself lost in the memory of a dream,

the singing hibiscus flooded my mind,

"how would she carry on, if I were to die here at Machon" I wondered,

for her and I had found a love in each other in the strangest of places,

at the most bizarre of circumstances,

the singing hibiscus, the strength that I needed to endure.

We had engaged the legions of Machon at sunrise, and before dusk the battle was over,

and we were defeated.

We had lost the battle,

but we had managed to get close enough to the red cathedral,

close enough to be heard by Samael, the left hand of god.

Helel Ben Sahar was dragged through the red blooded sands of Machon to the river Salsabil,

which fed water to the red cathedral and two other heavens.

Helel could see Samael, observing the proceedings of things from the height of the cathedral.

And as Agares bound the arms of Helel to the pillars of stone, Helel raised his gaze to Samael, whom he saw giving his approval to Agares to have Helel Ben Sahar executed,

"Any last words?" Agares the garrotter of the fifth heaven asked Helel Ben Sahar,

"yes, I have three" Helel replied,

and so the crowd was silenced so that Helel may have these, his final words;

I have Lilith, the dragon roared, "and if I die here, she dies as well."

...

At Shamayim the first heaven, after belial had extracted information of the whereabouts of Lilith, the trumpets of the assembly sounded, calling all fallen to the lunar cathedral,

"that can't be good" belial worried,

"Come on, let's go and hurry" she insisted.

However, as quickly as we tried to arrive at the assembly, the address was already over before our attendance,

"what's going on" belial quickly asked the angel Ezequael, who replied thus

"Azazel has ordered that we begin the march to the twin heavens immediately, as commanded by Helel Ben Sahar"

"and where is Helel Ben Sahar " belial asked, "I don't know" Ezequael replied, "no one has seen him since"

"and Azazel? " Belail questioned,

"he's at the forge, you'd find him with the smithereens,

"thank you Ezequael"

"let's go Nithael"

"what do you need me for"

I asked the archangel,

"I have already led you to Sansenoi"

"stop complaining and just hurry."

Soon we were at the forges and Azazel was there.

Azazel! Belail called,

"take a look at this", she showed him the amulet,

"Impossible" Azazel disbelieved,

"oh it's possible my friend"

"Who had this?" Azazel asked, "it was Sansenoi, he somehow managed to survive Samael"

"So he is alive?" "Barely" I replied the archangel,

"and you are?" Azazel furrowed as he turned to me,

"he's with me" belial responded,

" his name is Nithael, he found the angel with the amulet"

"good work brother" Azazel smiled as he complimented my actions,

" Thank you sir, that means a lot, coming from you.

"Did Sansenoi tell you what the amulet opens" Azazel turned to belial,

" yes he did, after much persuasion,

" and? "

"and he said that Lilith is locked away deep at the bottom of the ocean, the red sea to be precise and only with this, the amulet would the sea release her to us, the first woman.

"Wonderful news" Azazel rejoiced,

"With Lilith as our prisoner, we may not need to battle Samael at Machon, we could simply surrender to him the first woman and by her, buy our passage through the fifth heaven.

But who do we send to the sea to recover the woman,

"send us" belial offered, "no, I can't " Azazel refused, "I need you for the battle at Raquia and Shehaqim "

"Who do you have in mind?" Belial
asked,

"Arioch" Azazel answered,

"it took three angels to capture the
woman" belial reminded Azazel,

"you're right," he agreed, "so let us
send five instead, so that there would
be no mistakes.

Arioch would lead a team of Rimmon,
Ertael, Batarel, and Arakiel to the sea
and recover the woman Lilith,

and hopefully they would have
returned before the siege of Raquia and
Shehaqim was completed.

" Do you consent it belial, Azazel
asked the archangel,

"yes, I do" she agreed,

"They are a good pick."

...

As Samael from the height of the cathedral heard what Helel Ben Sahar had uttered, he was relieved and mad at the same time.

Helel! He yelled from the height of the cathedral as he glided down to the garrotter, and as he arrived there at the banks of the river Salsabil,

he handled the collar on the neck of Helel Ben Sahar and said

"I should break your neck myself" he threatened,

" do that and you'll never see your Lilith again" Helel replied,

"and how am I to be certain that you speak the truth Helel"

"I never lie Samael and you know that" Helel responded,

"you murdered two of the brethren on the account of Lilith,

but what about the third,

Sansenoi, you let him slip right through your fingers,

and your woman has suffered ever since, let my army through,

and I will bring your Lilith to you, so that you may ask her for forgiveness yourself."

"Fine Helel" Samael conceded,

" let us play this little game of yours,

but remember this,

if what you say are lies, I will hunt you down to whatever heaven you run, to whatever aid you find,

to whatever god that you may intercede, I will find you and kill you"

" I shall remember" Helel acknowledged Samael's threat.

Let them go, Samael commanded his powers, "but bring this one", he pointed to Helel Ben Sahar,

"bring this one to my cathedra, I wish to keep an eye on him myself.

And so one by one, we passed through the dreaded fifth heaven Machon into the white fields of Zebul.

And ss the fallen emerged one by one, Helel ben Sahar was now on his own,

and although the fallen rebelled,

we found ourselves praying to whomever wished to hear us,

for then, at that time, it was Helel Ben Sahar on his own, against the monster of heaven, and so we prayed that the monster would show mercy to the beast.

I have kept my word Helel,

Samael spoke, "where is my woman?"

" She is close" Helel replied

"and you will have her, once my last man has passed"

"my patience grows thin seraphim" Samael warned Helel Ben Sahar,

and as Samael still spoke, Arioch and his company came marching in to Machon,

and as they entered mars the streets grew silent, for the beauty of the woman Lilith was incomparable to the beauty of all that had after her been created,

such that words can not express it, and so I must not write of her beauty, only write that I could not write of it.

As silence blanked the red streets of Machon, Samael whispered, "she is here" and as he looked out through the balcony of the red cathedral,

the monster of heaven wasn't so much of a monster anymore,

as he fell to his knees on the blue of the marbled floors,

fighting back his emotions,

he turned to Helel and said "thank you"

and such was the shocking expression of gratitude from the angel Samael, that Helel Ben Sahar had no reply to offer the left hand of god but only say these,

"if it would please the lord of the fifth heaven, I wish to make one final request" Helel asked, "request it and I will grant it, however I can" "join us" Helel requested of the left hand,

"I can't "

"and why not?" Helel inquired, "you have suffered more than all the sons of heaven and yet you continue to serve, under the table, why?"

Helel urged the monster of heaven to reveal himself to him,

but Samael did not indulge the seraphim, he said nothing to him, nothing but

"I have been cursed by the incorruptibility Helel, never to leave this heaven,

I am not her lord this heaven, I am her prisoner,

I am not permitted to leave this place unless, leave to Zion and return"

"but if your shackles are removed, would you side with the fallen?"

"You can not break these chains seraphim, but if you would endure to Zion, then I may come to whatever end may follow.

CHAPTER TEN.

Michael, the one who is like god,

the lord of the fourth heaven,
Machonon,

a princely seraphim,

the archangel of protection.

At the time before the recrudescence
wars of the recreation,

Michael was known by another name,
"Rah" sun god,

a pagan god of the old Egyptian
peoples, until the incorruptibility sort
the sun god and offered him a renewed
purpose.

The sun god, like the others was hesitant of the incorruptibility and his promises,

and so he did not side with us in the beginning,

but the incorruptibility would not relent on a union with Rah,

and so he sent the entirety to convince the sun god,

but rah did not listen, and to Gabriel, Uriel, Anael, Mathael, and Cassiel, his answer remained the same.

"Who do I now send to the sun god rah? For I need him in the recreation of this world" The incorruptibility wondered,

" not Samael" he thought, "for he is more likely to blind the sun than guide it,

but Helel I shall send, the morning star and he shall deliver to me the sun"

and as the incorruptibility willed it, so it was.

Soon Helel ben Sahar arrived at the fourth heaven Machonon to convince the god of the sun rah to join in an alliance with the angelic host.

I hail thee, rah, sun god" Helel offered salutations to the deity and rah replied saying " I will tell you what I have told your god and the ones that came after him and before you"

"and what is that" Helel asked,

"I am not interested in your war" rah answered,

"we're not fighting a war" Helel replied, "and yet you gather an army?"

"We gather for peace to rebuild the world, one where there would be no pain or suffering"

the sun god laughed at the naivety of the seraphim,

"do you know how many times that I have heard those exact same words spoken?

Zeus spoke it before he murdered thousands, the titans and mortals alike,

Odin spoke it too and Jupiter, Shiva too and even the great spirits, *Wanka Tanka* and the lesser ones too, all who wish to recreate must first destroy, thus the wars,

and now you too speak of a recreation and you claim that you will not make war?

So please tell me godson, how would you buy this peace? "

I can't, Helel replied,

"all that I am permitted to say to you is that the incorruptibility has requested your hand by his side"

"that maybe good enough for the ones you have convinced to follow you godson,

but it is not good enough for me"

"forgive me" Helel pleaded,

"for I have failed to mention the promise we bring;

we would build a new celestial order, one that would be just and kind, strong and gentle too, where all who wish to worship shall worship and to those who do not, yet peace."

"And how do I fit in this plan of yours,

you can achieve all of these without my assistance"

"your design for the afterlife" Helel replied,

" and what about it" Rah asked,

"it is one that we intend to imitate for the mortals whom we shall guide, passage only to those who have lived right"

"and to those who have not" rah asked,

" other things" Helel replied.

I have heard you, Rah told Helel,

" allow me time to ponder on your offer,

I shall come to you, if I choose to be by your side,

"and we shall not come to you again with the bother of an alliance,

for I am the last that the incorruptibility shall send." Helel concluded.

Eight days passed and Rah did not come to the seraphim,

but then on the ninth day, after their
meeting,

at the arch of the crystal prism,

there was a golden ray that shinned
over the monument,

where Helel was

"who could this be" the seraphim
wondered,

and as the rays faded away,

Helel could see that it was the sun god
rah who had come

"you have come" Helel told the sun
god, "yes I have"

"What convinced you?" Helel asked,

"the potter" rah replied, "she convinced
me to follow the path"

"the potter?" Helel wondered,

"I have not met this deity before, and I know many deities if not all"

"do not worry on it Helel,

you will meet her soon",

"would you not now take me to the incorruptibility" rah requested,

"I shall" Helel replied,

"but you must first be reborn"

"reborn?" Rah questioned,

" yes reborn" Helel concurred,

"how do you mean" rah further questioned,

" your vessel" Helel replied,

" your vessel is unworthy of the brethren and Zion does not suffer the unclean,

if you must see the incorruptibility,

you must be reborn in the fires of purgatory,

you must become like the brethren"

"but you did not mention this before Helel" "I know and I am sorry for neglecting to do so" Helel offered the sun god his apologies,

"but it is however required by the trinity of the demiurge and for your own safety"

"my mind is made up" rah replied,

" show me the path so that I may follow it."

The rebirth shall occur at the fires of purgatory and from there,

those fires you shall be welcomed by the brethren.

And so Helel Ben Sahar opened a portal that led the sun god rah to the place of the fires where he was to become reborn by the baptism of fire.

As the sun god entered purgatory loud screams of pain escaped the inferno,

and through it all the seraphim Helel Ben Sahar was there to comfort the pagan god through the ordeal, and at the end, rah emerged from the inferno, bare from his head go his toes, he shined of gold and luminescent white, for he was the god of the sun, his feet were brown and golden like the sands of heaven and his hair was black like the blackness of the night, his mouth spat fire as he spoke and on his wings six consciousness carried him, but above all these, the sun god held a feature that no other in heaven possessed, not Helel, not Samael, and not Gabriel,

The sun god above him was a halo.

Such grace and rightly so,

for the sun god deserved the honour, for non was a god or a king among-st the brethren, non before rah, and as he stepped out beyond the inferno, the incorruptibility looked to him and said "the one who is like me, the one who is like god, '*Michael.*'

At the battle of the twin heavens Raquia and Shehaqim, Helel Ben Sahar was not with us, but soon before we marched for Machonon, the dragon returned and upon his arrival, the fallen rejoiced and dragon too was pleased, for we had overcome the twin cathedral, and even more so added to the satisfaction, the recovery of the long haired woman, Lilith, all was right with the fallen, and for a moment, it seemed as though we could do no wrong.

At the cathedra of the twin cathedral, Helel Ben Sahar celebrates with the fallen.

"My friends" Helel spoke to us,

"my friends, my brothers, my sisters, I have asked so much of you and always you amaze me with your dedication to the cause, no leader would ask for a better following. Shamayim, Raquia, and Shehaqim, fallen beneath our feet, burning by the strikes of our kindle, and if they..."

Helel paused, pointing his finger to the west,

"if they did not fear us before, they fear us now and by this disbelief,

we shall bring them all down, Machonon, Machon, Zebul and Araboth, and then, only then, shall all that has been promised be fulfilled.

Now I know that we have gathered to celebrate our mighty triumph, but if in our merry we forget the dead,

our brethren who have fallen, then we would have done them wrong in life and in death.

There is a song I know, but I can not sing it alone, for it drains by the burden of it's chorus,

so I urge you all to please brethren, sing it with me, let us bid the fallen farewell;

Morning has broken like the first morning, black bird has spoken like the first bird.

Praise for the singing, praise for the morning, praise for them springing fresh from the world.

Sweet the rain's new fall, sunlit from heaven, like the first dew fall on the first grass.

Praise for the sweetness of the first garden, spring in completeness where their feet passed.

Mine is the sunlight, mine is the morning, born of the one light Eden saw play.

Praise with elation, praise every morning, the brethren's who have so the brethren may live, praise.

As the tribute to the fallen came to an end, we celebrated wildly, for it was our first battle collectively as the fallen, and we were victorious.

Shortly after, morning came and the march to Machonon began,

and although the journey was short, it seemed as though the walk would never end,

as I could feel the piercing gaze of the archangel belial burrowing through my skull.

The archangel was still bitter from the night before, and I was afraid of what could follow.

Soon we arrived at Machonon, where every monument that stood was of gold and brass, vast monuments spread over the cover of dust, flowing through, beyond to the plantation of the laurels, beech, cedar and acacia.

This was my first time to the fourth heaven Machonon, and of all the wonders that I saw that day non was mightier than the Griffin, the guardians of the sun,

it had the body of a lion, the tail and back legs too and the head and wings were of an eagle, its front feet and talons too...,

"Wonderful" I admired the mighty beasts, " yeah right" Marou of the order of the cherubim's disapproved,

" they're not so special," he frowned as he walked away.

Something isn't right Azazel worried,
"yes I feel it too" Helel confessed,

"what do you think it is" Azazel asked,
"the Griffins" Helel replied,

" there's only one"

"do you think it's a trap to lure us in,

there are no guards at the gates either"
Azazel observed,

"it is unlike Michael to set traps" Helel
answered,

" even if you are certain of this, the sun
still is more quiet today than it has ever
been" Azazel responded,

"yes it is " Helel agreed,

"should we advance?" Azazel asked,
no, Helel refused,

" Let first the brethren rest as we send word to the lord of the sun".

Ready Amazarak and Abigor to enter Machon.

After the events that occur on the night before we arrived at Machonon, I avoided the archangel belial,

but soon she found me, at the shades of the laurels.

Are you avoiding me, she asked,

"of course not" I replied,

" I wouldn't, I couldn't"

"You're still not a good liar Nithael"

"I know" I replied, "we need to talk about what happened last night" "i was hoping that we wouldn't have to"

no, belial refused,

" it is better that we do, I need you to know Nithael that I drink a lot"

" I know that already" I told the archangel, "

I'm not done" she continued,

" I get carried away by free wine and making merry, and I know that last night when j spoke those words to you, you believed me drunk"

"but you were" I told the archangel,

" for a while yes, but at the end not so much"

"but I don't understand" I told belial,

" I was with you at the end"

"yes you were" the archangel replied, " goodbye Nithael and watch your back out there" belial concluded as she walked away.

At the night of the banquet I was confused, as my head wouldn't stop spinning at the euphoria of the impossibilities that the archangel had suggested, and now it spins even more.

CHAPTER ELEVEN.

Araboth, the city of god, Zion the cathedra of the incorruptibility. This was where we made our final stand, this was where the rebellion was to end . Here was where Helel Ben Sahar became the circle and truly the fallen.

We never stood a chance, not all of us by our numbers, not Helel Ben Sahar by his power, and so all became as it had always been intended.

Helel Ben Sahar, had asked the lesser brethren to sacrifice once, at the city of the red cathedral, the fifth heaven, but now here at the end, it is all of us who must lay down our lives, for the slender hope of victory.

At the twin heavens of Raquia and Shehaqim, Azazel had Organised the fallen into the legions that would now attack Araboth, but at that time we were twenty five thousand strong and five legions mighty, but after the battle at the twin heavens and the attrition at Machon our numbers were lessened, no longer five legions mighty, but only of three thousand and a quarter, mighty still, but not mighty enough, for all had gathered at Zion..., Machonon, Machon, Zebul and Araboth together as one under the command of Sachiel the lord of Zebul, with Michael the only brethren above the princely seraphim, looking down upon us all who were to perish, from great mountain of Zion.

At the end, I found myself trapped in a past, one not so long ago, only a few days old, my mind drifting to a time in the fourth heaven Machonon, when nothing else mattered except the memories of a moment.

I was badly wounded after the invasion of Machon, I couldn't remember much, only know that I was alive and the most beautiful of the angels tendered my wounds, "you're going to be okay" she said to me her voice, the assurance of confidence echoing in my head. I fell into a sleep by the softness of her hands and the soothing calm of her voice. I knew this angel, but I had not the wonder of imagination to know that her hands could heal so well. And as I awakened, she was there by the corner of my stand, "Nithael, are you awake?" She asked, " yes, I am" "I thought that we had lost you" " we?" I asked the angel, " I thought that I had lost you" she retold.

At Araboth, by the sounding of the trumpets, war!

Strategy was useless now, there were no plans that could upset the veracity of the fate that rained down upon us, only kill as many as you can, before the sword finds you as well, that was the strategy. Following the depletion in our ranks, I was reassigned to Belials command, thankfully we had reconciled our misunderstanding of the conjecture at Machon, and so she had my back as I had hers and together we revealed. Belial had always been possessed by rage, it was that, her edge over the twin lords of Raquia and Shehaqim, and rightly so, rage is required of the angel of lawlessness. But at the battle of the fallen, as it would come to be remembered, the archangel of lawlessness had lost her rage, and she fought by the possession of another emotion, one that I recognized, one far more impressive than the brief madness of rage.

At the seventh heaven Araboth, the power of the seraphim Helel Ben Sahar was unstoppable, but he could not become the beast here, for such was the holiness of the place Zion, that the dragon could not come.

Helel ben Sahar! Cassiel roared the dragon's name, challenging him to strike steel against steel. "You have disgraced our order" Cassiel accused Helel "and I can not bear to live, knowing that you as I breathe of the same air" "so what do you intend to do about that" Helel replied, " because I have no intention of dying today" "take a stand" Cassiel commanded "and let the steel decided who lives and dies" "priest of Zion" Helel called to Cassiel, "go back to Zion and slaughter the sheep, burn your incense and chant the Trisagion as you have always done, for that is the only thing that you know" "unshielded your weapon Helel and I will show you what I know" "you seek glory" Helel told Cassiel, "you believe that glory follows death? This is to be your oath fulfilled to the entirety, isn't it Cassiel" Helel called, " if I unshielded my blade from it's guard, I shall kill you here Cassiel, and on your way to the nothingness, you would realise, when it is all too late, that there is no glory in death" "then it would have been my lesson and not yours" Cassiel replied and as he unshielded his sword thunder struck at Zion as the heavens let down the rains and battered the fields. "So be it" Helel conceded to the chief of the seraphim's, as he too unshielded his weapon.

Leviathan as before at Raquia and Shehaqim, could not unlace himself, as he was yards ahead of the army, cutting down the once brethren like a shark in the waters. Before the lords of the seven heavens were designated, Leviathan, was the master of war and conflict, his sacrifices at the recrudescence wars of the recreation are legendary, he was to become the lord of the first heaven Shamayim, but he declined the offer, electing instead that Gabriel sit on the cathedra, and he Leviathan retired to the sea, until Helel Ben Sahar came knocking at the ocean.

Azazel had no quarrel with Leviathan's uncontrollable lust at the battle of the fallen, as he did at the twin cathedral, and so he did not caution the archangel, rather he urged his men to imitate the archangel. "Push forward!" Azazel commanded, "we must enter Zion" "Griffins!" A soldier on the lines alerted, " so this is where they brought them" Azazel confirmed, " cherubim's on me" he then commanded, "we must pull down those griffins, ready the nets and spears" he ordered.

At the peak of the mountain Zion, the archangel Michael remained, uninvolved with the struggles below, only observing from a height that only few could reach, and from that great height of the mountain he saw the dreaded monster of heaven Samael approaching from the west at a great speed. "Samael is coming" Marchosias, commander of the last legion warned the brethren, for if the left hand of god had come to stand against the fallen, then surely, this would be our end. And so the brethren by the entirety cheered as Samael arrived on the battlefield, as the fallen trembled In fear, but Samael had other intentions of his own, non that bothered the fallen, as he held a Griffin tightly on its wings and then with a blow, broke the beasts neck, Samael was on our side, but why, we wondered, perhaps it was the woman who had convinced him to come or perhaps he comes on his own accord.

Michael at Zion could not believe that the monster of heaven had turned against the entirety, and so to the Griffins by his side he commanded "fly down to Sachiel, and tell him to surround Samael, for he mustn't be allowed to interfere.

At the northeastern cardinal, Helel Ben Sahar forces an attack at the seraphim Cassiel, Cassiel fails to defend the blow and Helel delivers a deep cut, by the line off the side of the priest of Zion, "is this how you would defend your god?" Helel mocked Cassiel..., rattled by the dragon, Cassiel picks up his sword and charges at Helel Ben Sahar, he hits high, but Helel sees the incoming attack and block its well, so Cassiel hits low and Helel evades him by slithering to the his left hand side, Cassiel then lunges his sword at Helel, who turns against the projection of the blade, sweeping to the right of Cassiel and delivers a fatal blow to the high priest of Zion, blood spat from the mouth of Cassiel as a tear too dripped from his eyes and off his cheek, "I told you" Helel reminded the seraphim, "there is no glory in dying.

Belial get down, I quickly warned the archangel, as a Griffin dived to pick her apart, and as I warned her, she hurriedly rolled out of danger, "thank you, but we have to keep moving" "Belial!" Helel ben Sahar then called, " you need to reinforce Azazel and Marchosias in the middle, send word to Leviathan as well, forget the flanks, draw every man we have to the centre and spread, Samael is with us, and the brethren move to have him surrounded, we mustn't let that happen, if Samael is surrounded, we would have lost a great advantage, go now and hurry" Helel commanded, "flank off the centre, forget the lines" he repeated, " stick to Samael, I'll try my best to hold off the griffins ".

Berith! Belial then called, " did you hear Helel" "yes I did" he answered, " good, move the legions, two cohorts migrating from the right to the centre, westward and eastward, keep the movement tight, forward and defence until they reach the centre, we would hold this position until half of the legion is at the centre and then the rest would follow, do you understand? ``"yes I do" Berith confirmed, " then get moving ``" Nithael! Belial then called to me as well, "you're moving with the centuries of the first cohort to the centre now, do you understand?" She yelled, " no I declined, "I go when you go" I told her, " fool" Belial raged, "fucking virtue" she swore, " you'd die here" "then we shall die together" I told the archangel".

Maybe I was a fool, maybe we all were rebelling against the entirety, but I was never going to leave the archangel, for I knew that she was never going to leave me as well.

There were over one thousand two hundred Griffins in the air that day, at the battle of the fallen, a quarter of a legion, picking us off one by one, breaking our hold, line by line. We needed to concentrate on the war, and the nets and spears that Azazel had mobilised did little damage against the beasts that glided. Only by stopping their master, Michael would we overcome them.

And it was for that reason that the lord of the sun, chose the peak of Zion to command from, a height so great that even the archangels could not reach,

only the seraphim's and the cherubim's
could make the climb, an Ascension
that Helel ben Sahar had already
begun.

CHAPTER TWELVE.

At our first meeting, belial and I, I remember her singing the Dies Irae, "the day of wrath" on a heap of the dead, at Shamayim, it was a good song that day for truly there were many dead at Shamayim, and here now at the multiple meadows of Machonon, by the shades of the cedar and beech, she sings another, she sings to me of the rose of Sharon, she sings to the hibiscus.

"I am the rose of Sharon, a Lilly in the valleys.

Like a Lilly amongst thorns is my darling a amongst the maidens.

Like the apple tree amongst the trees of the forest is my lover among the young men.

I delight to sit in his shade and his fruit is sweet to my taste."

Belial concluded the chant and then she went on to say, "a millennia from now, a king named Solomon, shall have a vision of this place, the hibiscus, and he shall write this song, and sing it too, and the world would never know that I sang it firstly to you.

At the banquet of the twin heavens, the archangel belial seemed quite drunk, as she staggered drunkenly to the pillar of stone where I was, where I had hoped that she would not notice me.

"Hello Nithael" the archangel spoke, " why are you hiding behind that post" " I'm not hiding" I replied, " yes of course not, and I keel telling you that you're not a very good liar" "would you like to come with me" she then asked, " but the party's just begun" I replied, " there's no more wine" belial mourned, " the cellar was destroyed, a casualty of war" "but that doesn't mean that the celebration is over" "oh trust me" belial replied, " it is, any minute now, KASDAYE, would start singing and without wine to better, his awful tone, we would go mad" "but I don't think Helel would approve" I told belial, " Shh" belial responded with a shush, as it had become her habit to quiet me always, "don't think just follow and you're welcome" she continued as she firmly held to my arm and pulled me out of the cathedra, and as we exited the chamber, in a brief moment before we crossed the threshold, as belial had predicted, KASDAYE got up on a table and began to sing and of the first note that flew his lips, my ears if they could speak would beg for mercy.

After belial had pulled me away from the cathedral, we flew to the tower of the conjecture, a monument offered by Hermes and Aphrodite's to the entirety as a ransom to secure their passage through the recrudescence of the cosmos after Zeus's surrender at Zebul.

Thank you for getting me out of there, I happily told belial, " no need" she replied, " you didn't need to suffer" " no I did not, but thank you still." I told belial, as I engaged her in a conversation, "so tell me archangel, what is it like" "what is what like?" She replied, " being an archangel what is it like, to have all that power" "stressful" she answered, Ha, I tittered, " do you think that I'm being dishonest" belial asked, no, I replied at first and then yes I corrected, typical, belial sighed, "oh come on " I jeered the archangel angel, " how much stress does being an archangel come with? " but belial did not reply, "I'm sorry" I then apologized, " perhaps I was a bit insensitive, " there's no need to apologize" the archangel replied, " I like this look on you" "what look" I asked the archangel, " the look of freedom" she replied.

As the night progressed, belial and I spoke about many things, our hopes and expectations, and dreams as well, with the sweep of a moment, it felt as though we had known each other for many eternities. The archangel was beautiful, made perfect by the incorruptibility, the softness of her voice could sooth the worries of any mind. I had imagined unclean thoughts of the archangel, briefly at the conjecture, but I quickly returned to reason, however, I wouldn't have imagined that the archangel pondered on those thoughts as well had she not kissed me.

The moment was right at the tower, the stars were at their brightest, the wind was soothing and the silence calling. The archangel leaned in on me and placed a kiss gently on my lips, the world stood still, as I became helpless against the archangel, for I did not know how I was to react, but I knew that i mustn't indulge her, for it was against the ways of the brethren. "Please belial we mustn't" I halted the archangel, as I pulled reluctantly away, "why" she questioned, " say it is because that you do not feel the same way about me and I would you for your penance" " No" belial, I called softly to the angel, " I beg thee stop, for I fear that you wouldn't remember this moment in the morning after, as I could never forget it. You have had a lot to drink tonight, it would be shameful if I were to take advantage, you must forgive me" I begged the archangel, as I prepared to leave the conjecture, "and if I wasn't drunk?" Belial asked me hurriedly, before I departed, her voice broken by the cracking of a sob, "if you were whole, then k would not leave, I couldn't.

At the fourth heaven Machonon, Helel Ben Sahar had ordered a herald to the lord of the sun, Michael, hoping that the sun would agree to meet with Helel Ben Sahar and hear him out, as he once did when the now seraphim was the Egyptian deity Rah, but the forerunners returned as quickly as they had departed. The fourth heaven was abandoned, Michael was gone, and with him all the citizens of the sun, at the time of the revelation that the sun had been evacuated, I was at the plantation of the laurels, cooling in the shades, wondering of the night before, wondering on the archangel belial, and as my mind wondered on the kiss from the angel, I lost the balance of my emotions as my mind became unstable by the dreams of an illusion... Soon belial found me at the shades of the laurels, "Nithael" Belail called to me, "I have come tk say these to you and I wish for you not to speak only listen" "I drink a lot, and often I get carried away when the wine is free and the mood glee, but last night at the conjecture, I wasn't drunk and my emotions were not false". Belial told me, and she said no more except tell me that the fourth heaven had been abandoned by Michael, and that she would be at the palace of the seraphim Michael, the cathedral of the light, to wander.

My head had been spinning since the night at the conjecture, and now, it spins even more.

CHAPTER THIRTEEN.

At the final heaven Araboth, for a moment it seemed as though we could upset the hand of destiny and triumph at Zion. But of course, looks are always deceiving.

"Leave the griffins to me" Helel's parting words, as he began his ascension to Michael at Zion. And as the seraphim rose above the brethren on the battlefield, the beasts of the air sort to defend their master, picking off at the seraphim, one after the other, disturbing his ascent to the halo seraphim. On the battlefield, the brethren did not notice Helel ben Sahar's struggle with the griffins in the air, until he came crashing down hard at Araboth.

"Leviathan! Where is Leviathan" Helel asked, as he steadied himself, after the fall, "where is Leviathan" Helel asked Reeba, the brethren closest to him, "I don't know" she replied, "but Azazel should" she told the seraphim, " and where is Azazel? " "at the center" she replied, and so at once Helel Ben Sahar hurried to the archangel Azazel.

Arriving at Azazel's command, Helel Ben Sahar asked the archangel, " where is Leviathan" he yelled, "northwest, left flank forward" Azazel yelled back, "what? Why?" Helel raged, "he doesn't listen" Azazel replied, " he's outpacing the army and I cannot control him" "no, we can't" Helel agreed, " but we can unleash him" he told, " I need to bet to Michael, but I cannot get passed the griffins" Helel informed Azazel, " you need the angels that can make the climb and I cannot make that climb nor leave the army without a commander" " so what do you suggest that I do now" Helel asked Azazel, " take Leviathan, I reckon that's why you seek for him, take Arioch and Marou too, they're good soldiers and they follow orders well" Azazel told the seraphim, "Arioch, Marou" Azazel then called, " Helel Ben Sahar needs you" he ordered, " hold them together brother" Helel then said to Azazel, " for this battle would not end shortly" " I know" Azazel replied, " I know " he repeated.

Shortly after Helel Ben Sahar left the center where Azazel was stationed, Marchosias came calling, " Azazel, we need to cut down Sachiel, he's causing us all sorts of problem at the left center, "are you mad" Azazel disapproved, " don't you see the legions that surround him?" "I do" Marchosias replied, " that's why we need to cut him down, to break his command" " there is no way that we can get close enough to him" "no, we can't, but Samael can" Marchosias suggested, " no" Azazel refused, " we need Samael at the center, if he leaves..., the line breaks" "then who goes? Who van match the power of a seraphim" Marchosias asked Azazel, " I don't know" he replied, "there is no brethren I know mad enough to challenge the lord of the sixth heaven" and as the archangels continued to contemplate on a strategy for battle, belial was gored by the cherubim Asilious, who had the head of an ox and the body of a rhino on the wings of an angel. And as he propelled the archangel through the air, she landed at the feet of the angels AZAZEL and Marchosias, and together, at the same time, they called, "belial".

"Belial" AZAZEL and Marchosias called the archangel, " what?" She responded, as she recovered from her fall, " we need someone to engage Sachiel" Marchosias told the archangel, "what?" Belial again blared, " are you both mad" she accused the archangels, " Sachiel is a fucking seraphim" belial further replied, " so is that a no?" Marchosias asked, " yes, that's a fucking no" "send Samael" she then told Azazel, " no, we can't, he's needed here at the center" "have you seen the legion surrounding Sachiel, there is no way that I could get close enough to the hairless lord of the sixth heaven, even if I wanted to, they're too many of them" belial warned, " and we don't have the men to break them" Marchosias added, " but what if we could break them" AZAZEL asked the archangels, " would you engage

Sachiel?" He further questioned, " I ca not promise victory over the lord of Zebul, but I will fight him, if I get a chance" belial replied, " "as will I" Marchosias too offered himself to battle the lord of Zebul, " but we would need a miracle to get over these lines and engage the lord of Zebul" belial told "and a miracle yet to defeat him" Marchosias too replied, "then let us make that miracle happen" Azazel told the brethren, "get behind me he then commanded, as he focused his gaze westward, at the standing of Sachiel.

What's the plan, Arioch asked Helel Ben Sahar, as they parted the wind to the Griffins above, "you know Leviathan and I can not make that climb" Arioch told the seraphim, " yes

I know brother" Helel replied, " I only
need your help to get passed the
griffins, then Marou and I would carry
on to Michael, " a seraphim, one
cherubim and two archangels, against a
quarter legion of griffins, I like our
odds" Arioch told the seraphim, " yes
brother me too" Helel Ben Sahar
replied, " me too" he repeated.

At the seventh heaven Araboth, it is
forbidden for the unclean to enter this
place, the unworthy were by the
heaven itself cast away by fire and
lightening. Such is the holiness of the
place, such is the power that dangles at
Zion, the power that dangles over the
rebellion. And so Helel Ben Sahar
could not become the dragon here, else
he'd be struck down by a blaze of fire

and lightening, and yet Azazel considers this drastic sacrifice to aid the fallen, the advantage we needed to take down the lord of the sixth heaven Sachiel.

Get behind me, Azazel commanded the brethren, "behold the miracle" he the then told, "what miracle? " belial wondered, "the miracle of a sacrifice" Azazel replied, as he transformed himself into a hideous monster, stretching many meters through the blooded fields of Araboth, almost reaching Zion, to where Sachiel commanded from, before lightening blasted the commander of the first legions, Azazel, and then followed the fires. "No! Marchosias cried, as he realized too late what the archangel had intended, and was unable to stop him, as he watched him become obliterated to dust and ash by the fire and lightening of ZION. "He sacrificed himself" belial whispered, as she lost herself to the horror of the archangels death, but quickly she recovered, as it was her nature, "here's our chance" she hurriedly urged Marchosias, "sachiel is injured" belial observed, as the blast of lightening from above caught little of Sachiel as well. Azazel had drawn close enough to the seraphim, ensuring that the brethren had the miracle he had promised.

CHAPTER FOURTEEN.

Amare et sapare vix concetidur; To be in love and to be wise is scarce, granted even to a god.

At the shades of the laurels on the plantation of the sun, the Archangel BELIAL had left my head spinning like the wheels of a chariot as she headed for the cathedral of the light.

At the slaughter of Machon all that I could think of was the singing hibiscus, on the night before she sang, on the morning before the March.

And to those things that I dream of now never have the thoughts been spoken, never these dreams been dreamt or such a will be dared, but here on the plantation of the sun, I dare to dream such a dream, that a virtue could love an Archangel and that she too could love him back.

At the garden of the cathedral, across the lake of the golden larva the Archangel BELIAL waited. "At las you came" she said to me as she sensed my presence, "I could not stay away" I confessed to her, as she drew closer to my standing "I'm glad that you are here Nithael" she said to me softly, but I was lost for words, as she reached for my arms and locked deep into the faze of my eyes, my tongue failed me, as it chose silence over words.

"And if it should kiss you now… again, Nithael! Need I ask for a penance afterwards" "No! For it is I that shall ask for the penance, for I wish to kiss the angel one more time" I told the Archangel as I now held her firmly by the arm which she had held me, pulling her closer to my bearing as I continued to gaze deep into the hue of her eyes and then, there, under the night of the sun I kissed the archangel of lawlessness and then the dream.

Several times I had described the archangel Belial as deceptively beautiful, soft in voice and above all else inexpressibly wicked, but as I laid with her at the gardens of the cathedral beyond the river if gold and larva, it dawned on me that "oh how wrong I have been" for now in my judgement as it comes to my conscience, the

Archangel BELIAL beautiful without compare, always soft in tone and kind with an unusualness that comes misunderstood by the position of her tittle.

Her lips were soft and gentle like a breeze drifted far from the harshness of the seas and tender too like a morning dew, dripping off the curving of a gardens green.

Before the night that we shared at the gardens we first shared a moment at the tower of the Conjecture, then I had always worried of consequences, but as my lips net with here that night at the sun… consequences be damned.

BELIAL was always in armor and not only by the strappings of the titanium on her back and breasts, but also by the confiscation of her emotions, she was always on the defense, never wanting to be vulnerable, never electing to be weak. But as the strappings of the metals fell off of her piece by piece and we were both bare from the brown silky fullness of her hair to the pink coated sole of my feet, there was nothing at the place of the gardens to defend against , and so the Archangel BELIAL let go of armor, body and soul

And so, I laid her down on the white and yellow ox-eyed daisies, and then on top of her too I laid, kissing her arms slowly, steadily climbing to her shoulders, brushing her skin gently with the softness of my lips and then to her neck I arrived and by a mild nibble I dug on her and she let out a sigh that warmed beneath the lob of my ear, by the side of my cheek, barely above the chip of my jaw and then followed a deep long breath as she called to me "Nithael! What happens tomorrow" she whispered to my ears, "for there is that chance that neither of us would live to see this war ended" and so I whispered back to her "to the one that lives or dies, this moment here, now should he and her hold dearest until whatever end may come" I comforted her as I stared at all of her glistening body and her soul, from the hue blue sparkles of her eyes, to the slightly hollow dimple on her cheek, the short curly lashes on her kids, the waving contour of her breasts by the pink luscious temptations of her nipples, the symmetry of her hips to her body, the perfection, the desire, the admiration and memories that I would never forget. And as I gazed at her, Belial, from the top of her head to the bottom of her feet and then back again the sparkle of her eyes she said to me "let us make love, so that these memories shall forever be complete and never lacking in all of its excesses" a request that not even a god may resist.

So, I kissed her again, and then kissed her by the side of her breasts teasing her nipples by the scrubbings of my lips as her hands rubbed gently on my back, her fingers roaming on the perspiration on my skin, parting the

roots of my hair at the base of my neck
and then when the moment was right
and the chipping of the crickets grew
silent I took her, deep but gentle and
then deep again and again but not so
gentle anymore, and by every stroke
that I pulled she let out a broken moan
that stuttered like a broken flute
missing a key by the error of the piper
as her fingers dug deep beneath the
cover of my back, holding on firmly as
she anchored me by the curving of her
legs and feet, ensuring that every thrust
was proper and firm to the depths that
she desired.

We rolled over the daises, the
dandelions, vetches and the hawkbits
too, our bodies picking up the floral
yellows and purples, blues and whites,

red and greens as well of the cathedral gardens, by the perspiration of our bodies. And when neither could hold the excesses of the passions that burned we came to a halt at the row of the purple vetches and there we laid until k the morning, the morning when she sang to me the hibiscus, the rose of Sharon, by the floral coatings of the night before still clinging to her body and by the rays of the yellow sun the Archangel BELIAL was transformed from that which she was to a goddess of the nymphs. Freedom was the choice that I sort, freedom was why I joined the rebellion, but now here at the gardens of Machonon, I would sacrifice that freedom for more moments like these, for moments with the singing hibiscus.

Chapter Fifteen.

He made it, Helel Ben Sahar made it to the space in between spaces, the dwelling place of the entirety, surely now, the fallen can hope.

At the space in between spaces, Helel Ben Sahar comes face to face with the entirety.

"Helel" the entirety called to the seraphim "I have been expecting you, you have been through a lot, perhaps you wish to rest first, for a while before we speak?" "Do you know why I am here?" Helel questioned the entirety "Yes I do, you are here now and it will all be over soon, do not be afraid Helel" the entirety continued "Here time is irrelevant, it is non linear here, it is only where or when I want it to be. Rest now and then come to me and I shall aid you to destiny" "I have not come here by the calling of destiny " Helel told the entirety "of course not" the entirety agreed "You have come by the calling of freedom, or am I incorrect?" the entirety asked, a question to which the seraphim remained silent.

Destiny is as malevolent as the greatest of evils and so to those who surrender to the will of fate become mindless disciples to a maniacal master and to those who resist her, she still arrives at the cross roads of the soul. The malevolent true nature of destiny is often disguised by the benevolent ingenuity of a grandeur plan where every sacrifice is misinterpreted to a purpose and every purpose is feigned to suit the deceivability of a lie. We are slaves all of us, the divine and the mortal alike to a master who cares little for the little and even lesser for the mighty. There is no purpose to the pain, there are no plans for the suffering, only a hand making vases in a darkness breaking the vases made as she searches for the clay on the potter to spin again. Destiny is a blind potter, molding in the darkness, cracking the vases to find the clay.

"I am rested" Helel returned to the entirety, "Yes you are" the entirety acknowledged the seraphim. "I know what you would ask Helel, but ask it still so that I may refuse it yet." " If you know then why need I ask" Helel Ben Sahar asked, "So that the moment would have been lived and no longer linger in the nothingness of time."